Bone Sliver

The Nova Wave: Book 1

D.E. Chandler

To Sandy,
Stay Human!

D.E. Chandler

Published By Twisted Candle Media
Sapulpa, OK

ISBN: 978-0-9965524-0-0

Cover by Travis Miles at Probookcovers.com. Author photo by Ian Mildon Photography.

Thanks!

If I were to thank everyone who helped to make this first book possible, it would take up enough room for another whole chapter, so I'll start with the closest to center. I'd like to thank my parents, all of them, but especially Daddy. You told me I could be anything I wanted, and you were right. I'd like to thank my husband, Tom. Your patience and support have meant everything. I love you.

Special thanks go out to Lonnie R. Brown, whose character Kane Quinn makes frequent cameos in Max's world. He was just the kick in the pants Max needed.

To all of our friends and family who suffered through the early stuff, provided feedback, and still managed to read it again (You know who you are...) you are amazing. You all sure know how to make a girl feel special.

Thank you all.

D~

ONE

(2045)

"Horseshit."

I held the mini mag between my chattering teeth, trying to read the notes on my first report for 2017. I glanced again over the penned-in comments at the bottom of the page.

One read, "Maxwell Edison, field agent, has repeatedly flouted the bylaws of this institution and disregarded orders. As such, I am recommending immediate disciplinary review. Undersecretary G. Chamberlain."

Another read, "Though his actions seem erratic sometimes, Agent Edison is effective in the field, and has repeatedly shown himself to be an asset to this office." That one wasn't signed. I wondered who wrote it, but the gently looping script gave me a couple of ideas.

I crushed the report and tossed it into the passenger side floorboard. If it came down to a choice between a raise and a pink-slip, there wasn't much question which one I was going to get.

There'd been no activity at the faded red-brick building I'd been watching for two days, and I was getting the impression there wasn't going to be any. I really had to piss. I sucked down the last of my ramen soup, and then pitched the empty paper cup into the floorboard as well. When I opened the white pickup's one primered door, the frosty air assaulted my exposed face and hands. My breath seemed to explode from my mouth in great puffs of steam. Now I really had to go.

I crawled out and slammed the door so it would stay closed. Man, I missed my Mustang.

I tucked my thermal shirt into my jeans, buttoned up my old denim jacket and flipped the collar up around my ears, letting the graying brown hair that hung like moss around my shoulders act as insulation. I pulled the old sock hat out of my pocket and put it on, then stuck my hands in my pockets. It wasn't real warm, and I probably looked like a bum, but it kept the wind out.

I didn't want to take a chance of someone finally showing up just to find me taking a piss beside my truck, so I hiked down the street a couple of blocks, sticking to the shadows under the brushy, overgrown fence-line. I found a grassy spot in an alley behind a dumpster about a block away. Since everything around me was locked up tight, I decided to relieve the pressure.

That mission accomplished, I set out for the relative warmth of my truck. When I turned the corner back onto the sidewalk, I bumped into the biggest, ugliest man I'd ever seen. And for a guy who's seen plenty of pissed-off grunts from all over, that's saying something. Our collision knocked me off my feet, sprawling me ass-first into the street.

He grunted. The lumbering mountain of a man looked at me with a thin smirk scrawled across that stony jaw. Above it hung a nose that looked like it had seen a few too many right hooks. He just grunted at me and lumbered on. Glancing ahead of him, as I got my feet under me, I realized there was someone up there he was following.

Someone tiny, maybe five foot, in a hoodie and a mini-skirt.

She hopped the bar to the mini-storage across the street and ducked around a corner and he followed. The idea of that monster catching up with her, and what might ensue after, made my skin crawl. I didn't like the idea of anyone in pain, I'd seen enough suffering to last me a lifetime. The fact that it was a girl-- that made my blood boil, so I followed them into the maze of the mini-storage.

I'd spent eight long years in the Marine Corps, and in all that time, my instincts about people had never failed me. When I peered around the corner, though, I realized that tonight they had.

The man-mountain was prone on the asphalt, and the tiny female advanced on him, her hands held out in an arc that made it look like she was holding an invisible ball.

His great mallet-like fists hung over the top of his head, as his arms covered his face. I could see him shaking, even from my corner. The little gal reached him at last, and she just laid her hands on either side of his head. He howled, his shaking form now writhing.

I felt my guts twist and my face screw up, but I couldn't look away from the big guy agonizing under the little woman's touch. I willed my legs to move. I had to get in there, but I couldn't. I was glued to the spot. Should I even try? If she could take down that guy, what could she do to me?

Shit, Max, grow a pair, boy! You grow a yellow stripe after you got back? What the hell are you scared of? You've been a dead man since you enlisted. Ooh-rah. I forced my legs to carry me around the corner.

Once I stepped around the corner, I saw her head snap up in my direction. The big guy's pale, unmoving eyes stared up into the blackness, and I was pretty sure he was dead. The little woman leapt over the prone body and came right at me.

"Shit fire." I said quietly. Looking around for some cover and not finding any, I ducked back around the corner, unholstering my trusty Colt .45. I got low and aimed around the corner, hoping to corner her before she ran past me. When I brought the weapon down along the wall, she was waiting. She kicked my hand hard, knocking it against the cinder block wall.

A gut-wrenching pain shot through my hand, into my arm and shoulder, causing me to lose my grip. The gun clattered away on the pavement.

She'd closed the space between us while I was focused on the pain and the loss of the weapon. She was between me and the gun now, so close I could smell her perfume-- something woody and musky. Before I could react, she reached for me.

It's amazing how much you notice when you're completely screwed. When she reached for me, her hood fell back and I could see her face. She was young, maybe twenty, short and thin with spiky orange-red hair and hazel green eyes. Those eyes darted back and forth behind their heavily mascara laden lashes so fast she could have been reading a binary feed screen. She seemed to be assessing me. There were piercings in her nose and lower lip, but they were tastefully subtle and attractive on her.

"You didn't see me," she said, "I was never here."

I remember vaguely thinking *bullshit*, before the tiny hands gently touched my cheeks. The whole world seemed to tilt sideways and then-- I *was in Iraq, on the ground outside our caravan after the explosion. I was crawling, trying to reach BB before he bled out without getting killed myself. There was a pain in my chest, but I had to keep moving. I finally got to him, and tried to apply pressure, but the warm, sticky liquid just kept pulsing up between my fingers. He couldn't talk, and he couldn't breathe. The rest of the mayhem seemed to fade then, and all I could hear were the gurgling sounds my buddy was making, just trying to get a breath. I tried to breathe for him, willing the air into his lungs. All I could smell was smoke and burning flesh and rubber. BB-- he finally quit trying. The blood slowed and finally ceased. I leaned back against the truck he'd fallen out of, my own pain suddenly very real. I coughed. The only reason I even knew I was coughing blood was because there were new red spots in the relatively clean places on my trousers.*

BB was dead. The other two from my vehicle were dead. I'd failed BB and now I was going to die, too. I could feel it now. It felt as if there were two pieces of shrapnel. One was hovering right in my ribcage, just below my left clavicle, and another a little deeper and lower had gone in under my arm, near my heart. That one had likely punctured a lung, and maybe damaged my heart.

When I came to, the woman was gone, and I had no idea how long I'd been out. My chest still hurt, but I clambered to my feet and walked over to the big guy. I retrieved my .45 on the way, and as I got closer, I could see his eyes were open, still and staring. There wouldn't be a pulse, but I had to check anyway.

When I reached down to check him, he was already stiff. I recoiled, the unnatural chill of his body seeming to invade my joints. It wasn't that I hadn't seen death, obviously, but something about this guy dying the way he did really got to me. Whatever whammy she'd put on this guy killed him. She probably could have killed me, as well. I wondered what all she could do with that touch as I retrieved the cell phone from my pocket and speed-dialed The Office.

"Office, Toni."

At the sound of her voice, the tension from tonight's events began to ease out of my shoulders. "Hey, Toni," I said wearily, "How's the most angelic devil in the world?"

"Max," she said, her voice flat, "What have you got for me?"

I took a deep breath. No matter how much weird shit happened to me, it never got any easier reporting it, even after five years.

"Okay, teeny little chick takes out a six-foot-five galoot with a single touch and doesn't leave a mark on him. Oh, and she attacked me, too."

"Gods! Are you okay?"

"Yeah. Rattled though, I think I'm done for the night."

"You said rattled. Tell me."

"She did something to my head and I had the mother of all flashbacks."

"Like a PTSD one?"

"Yeah, but way worse than any I ever had. Usually it's just visual, or at worst visual and auditory, this was all five senses. I was there. I was in Iraq." Talking about it, I could feel that tension creeping back in, and my heart rate quicken. The scar under my arm itched insanely, and suddenly the night's chill was more biting again.

"I'm so sorry, Max," she said, her voice softening with real concern, "Why don't you come in and we'll send someone down to cover for you for a while?"

"No, I'm alright," I said, leaning back against the wall to help steady my body and my nerves. "I need to stick here and find this chick. See where she goes and who she's attached to."

"At least take someone with you, we have five agents there right now, including you. Take Claire."

"Damn, Toni," I said pushing off the wall, "The last thing I need right now is someone else to look after."

"Max, Roosevelt would be rolling over in his grave if he knew you guys were out there solo anyway. Something is building up down there, and you can't afford to freefall right now. And besides, she'd be looking after you."

"Founders be damned," Toni was gorgeous, but she was starting to piss me off. "I don't need a babysitter. You're not my boss, and you're not my girlfriend. You're a glorified dispatcher, so don't try to pull rank."

"Whatever, Max. I'm sending Claire to find you, and Shane and Eric to clean up. Can you give me a location?"

I clenched my jaw and said, "Yeah the body's in an alley off of Lewis, about three blocks south of The Dreammaker Lounge. I'll wait for them to get here, but they better hurry, it's fucking cold."

"Fine." She hung up.

I guess I pissed her off, but it never got back around to me. When the guys showed up to collect the body, I started the walk back to the truck. I didn't need her hanging another partner around my neck right now. As far as I was concerned, partners were only guilt magnets, and I had plenty for one lifetime. I got in the truck and started it; grateful I could turn the heater on and warm up a little. I hooked a right on Lewis to head back North; I had a date with a bottle named Patron.

The Dreammaker Lounge was just as beautifully loud and smoky as I remembered bars being before they banned smoking in most places. I found my usual spot at the end of the bar unoccupied, and assumed the barfly position. I tried not to make eye contact with anyone but the bartender. I kept remembering what the doc had said to me after my surgery.

"One-one-thousandth of an inch," he'd said. The shrapnel that had lodged in my ribcage was metal, but the piece that almost punched my card wasn't. It was a piece of bone from one of the guys in the Humvee with BB and me.

I did have a glance or two at the short stage where a pair of tall blondes with matching-- everything in red sequined halter tops were singing "Delta Dawn". It was always Karaoke night at the Dreammaker Lounge.

The bar's matron, in her black lace bolero and sequined dress cut a striking figure against the reflected neon in the back mirror as she oversaw the comings and goings from behind the bar. Something about her reminded me of my ex. Maybe it was the hint of accusation in her eyes as she caught sight of me. It was a momentary contact, but her judgment was completed instantly. I caught sight of myself in the mirror and decided she was probably right. I did look like a bum.

I looked older and more tired than my forty- one years should have allowed. I took off the sock hat and stuck it back in my pocket and turned my collar back down. It helped, but not much. My hair was lank, disheveled and dirty. The eyes of a stranger stared back at me.

The bartender slid a napkin in front of me, and I met his eyes.

"Patron," I said, as if I needed to.

The young man nodded and turned, retrieving a double shot glass and the bottle. That done, he took out a marker and made two marks on the bottle, then set it and the shot glass in front of me. One of the marks was where the liquid was now; the other was where he would have to cut me off. Apparently *he* remembered last time. That sucked.

I tried to put the pieces together from the last several anomalous encounters I'd had. Toni had said that something was building up, but what? I'd seen too much to count out anything at this point, and not enough to really understand what was going on. If I was going to get anywhere, I was going to have to find the girl.

For now though, I had to shut down the gears in my head so I could sleep. I poured my first shot and let the firewater do the magic it was so famous for. The tequila burned, but its warmth quickly spread through me, soothing away all of the memories, all of the questions, and soon anything that resembled conscious thought. Now, *that* I could believe in.

TWO

Rolling into a consciousness that hurt everywhere, I popped open an eyelid to take in my surroundings. Bad move. Skull-splitting light invaded the open eye and made the pain in my head worse than all the other pain. I didn't remember coming in, and come to think of it, I didn't remember that painting in my motel room.

A woman's voice drifted in from the bathroom. She was singing. *Aw, fuck.* I sat up, looking around for my clothes. There was a moment of mild panic when I didn't see them anywhere. A wave of nausea clenched my gut and I immediately lay back, trying not to hurl.

I'm getting too old for this shit. I squeezed my eyes closed for a minute, and when I opened them again, I realized I still had my clothes on. The bathroom door in the cheap motel room swung open, assaulting me with still more skull-splitting light, and I instinctively pulled up the covers before I remembered that I had my clothes on and relaxed.

Claire Reynolds stepped out and flashed me one of her amazing smiles. A hot flash of guilt mingled with intrigue sailed from my brain to my groin and back again in a space smaller than a nanosecond. *Nah, I wouldn't. She wouldn't. Would she?*

Claire had her long blond hair done up into a tight braid that hung out the back of her pink camo baseball cap, all the way down to the embossed leather belt she wore around her faded jeans.

"G'mornin', sunshine!"

"Hey," I said, hoping it sounded better and less grating outside my head.

"You look like cold shit on a hot plate," she said, her blue eyes scanning me.

"That's kind of how I feel too. Hey, what happened last night?"

At that question, a mischievous glint lit those eyes and her smile adopted a much more sensual form.

"Well," she said, "I found you, stoned on Patron and making an ass of yourself. When I tried to talk you down, you swept me off my feet, kissed me crazy and I brought you back here and did terrible, wicked, wonderful things to your body," she said, her backwoods drawl not helping at all. "Would you like me to demonstrate?"

She put a knee on the edge of the bed and leaned in close. The she reached up with one hand and touched my cheek. Then she smacked me. Not hard, just enough to break the spell of her words.

"I talked you down," she said, her voice returning to her usual tone and habit, "And I brought you up here to sleep it off, you yo-yo. You passed out in the car and I had to drag your dead-drunk ass up the stairs. You slept. That's all."

"Oh thank God," I said, only half relieved, "I mean-- not thank God because of you, but because of me. I mean..."

"Shut up Max."

"Okay."

A thunderous boom interrupted the awkward silence between us, followed swiftly by the sound of shattering glass and a momentous cracking sound. The cheap hollow-core door flew off its hinges. It flipped a time or two and nearly took off Claire's head on its way to smash against the back wall.

I grabbed her arms and pulled her down. I rolled with her off of the bed and onto the floor. The door just caught the tip of the braid trailing behind her head. Car alarms were going off.

After an even more awkward moment, I let go of Claire's arms and we headed for the gaping doorway. I grabbed my jacket and shoes on the way. We stood in the opening gazing out onto the destruction below as I shook the broken glass out of my jacket and put it on.

"My car," she said, "Somebody blew up my car."

"Who did you piss off?"

"Only people I've killed or put away. And maybe my ex, but he's also in jail."

"One of them must have gotten out," I said, leaning against the naked doorjamb and slipping my shoes on.

"How would they know where I am?" She cuffed me on the shoulder and said, "What if it's you? Who'd you piss off?"

"Everybody else." Despite the mayhem I couldn't help the grin that I could feel creeping across my face. "How far from the bar are we?"

Claire looked up at me. Her eyes must have been watering from the smoke as she said, "About a half a mile east and a block north. Hey, you don't need to go back there and start in again."

I put my hands up in a show of surrender and said, "Just going to get my truck. It looks like you're riding with me for now."

"Glorious," she said. *Has she seen me drive?*

"If you'll wait here," I said, listening to the sirens approach, "I'll go get it and be right back."

I stalked down the breezeway, and just as I reached the stairs down to the parking lot, I could see a slim figure through the smoke. A person in a hoodie. *The girl from last night?* I rattled down the stairs quickly. The person was still there when I reached the bottom.

Avoiding eye contact, I headed toward the street, hoping to at least get a better look. I kept the person in my peripheral as I turned the corner onto the sidewalk. Whoever it was wore a gray hoodie and faded gray jeans.

I walked quietly, keeping an ear out behind me. I didn't hear her, but I could swear I felt her eyes on me. I couldn't be sure, but I didn't really want to let her know I was looking, so I crossed the street, giving me an excuse to look both ways. *There she is.* Now that I knew she was tailing me, I'd let her follow me to the bar and see if I couldn't get her to tell me what the hell happened last night.

A couple of blocks later, I crossed Lewis to be on the west side of the street with the bar and turned south when I reached the corner. Sure enough, she was still there. I hoped she wouldn't chicken out. She was either looking to finish the job from last night, find out more about me, or explain-- maybe. Either way, I needed to get her to talk to me. If she was part of my anomaly, and if she was the one who blew up Claire's car, I had to find out.

The bar had been open since eleven o'clock, so I went straight in. The bar's matron was nowhere to be seen this morning, but the bartender from last night scowled good morning at me. It was strange seeing the bar in daylight. The dark colors and plastic lights that looked so cool lit up at night, were tired and garish in the late morning sun. I didn't take my usual stool at the bar, opting instead for a better vantage point to see whether she came in after me.

I went to the U-shaped booth in the far corner, slipped my jacket off and laid it in the red plastic covered seat as I slid in, and then looked up to order. I'd thought the waitress was behind me, waiting to take my order, but it was her. She was already there.

Her sudden appearance had startled me, but I knew better than to show it. Until I knew what her angle was, I had to consider her a threat.

I made my face a mask, but her gaze unsettled me inside. The hazel-green eyes were as penetrating as I remembered, peeling away layers of will and laying bare my soul. They touched someplace deeper, tenderer. The place I kept well-guarded. *She has me, and there will be no escape unless she wills it. Bullshit, she's just a girl. Watch those hands, though. She's a killer.* Anyway, she had me right where I wanted her.

She broke the gaze momentarily, and my mind cleared. I opened my mouth to ask her who the hell she was and what happened, but she lifted one of those hands. The movement made my insides squirm, and I hoped it wasn't visible. Eyes flashing, she put a finger to her lips. They curved into a little smile.

Here I could see her more clearly. There were fine red freckles across her cheeks and nose. Her cheekbones were high and her chin pointed, giving her face a definite heart shape. The effect with the short red hair was pixie-like.

"Shh," she said, "I'm not who you think I am."

The other hand moved, coming out of her hoodie pocket with a business card. She laid it on the table, keeping it covered with that tiny, terrifying hand.

"Don't follow me," she said. Then she removed the tiny hand from the card and strode out the door.

She was already at the door by the time I snagged my jacket and swiped the card off the table, sliding out of the seat behind her. *To hell with "Don't follow me."* If she could follow me, I was damn well going to follow her. Besides, if she got away, she would be a pain in the ass to find again.

I was quick, but she was quicker. She was almost out of view around the corner at the end of the block when I caught sight of her. I sprinted, but had to jump the legs of a tall, thin old man sitting on the sidewalk, with his possessions gathered around him, and then I had to duck around a young couple pushing a stroller. She was already turning down the alley before I got to where she'd turned.

Girl can run! Damn, I've got to get back in shape.

Winded, I walked to the alley she'd ducked into. She was nowhere to be seen. I stopped, listening for any sound in the alley itself, or for footfalls anywhere. It was hard to hear anything but the sound of my own breathing.

There was a dumpster on either side of the alley, several back doors and two more corners to turn at the end. I walked to the end of the deserted alley, looking for something that might tell me which way she went.

I went down the alley, contemplating this last of my many failures, and checked the dumpsters and checked all the doors along each building. All were locked. Either she'd gone in one and locked it, or she'd kept running. Reaching the end I looked around the corners in both directions. The right one led back around to a street after a series of empty back parking lots, and the left just ran along the other side of the building, with a big field across from it.

As I walked, I scanned the bits of accumulated dirt and mud in my field of vision. If she'd left a footprint I didn't want to miss it. I looked up the fire escapes. I still felt like someone was watching me, but there was no one to be seen.

With her lead and her speed, I'd never catch her. Claire was waiting. I trudged back to the bar but didn't go in. I got in my Ford and started the engine. While I let it warm up, I stuck the business card she'd given me into my jacket pocket and checked the back seat to make sure my duffel bag was still there. It was safe and sound, so I proceeded to stuff an old Great-Mart bag with the accumulated trash from my three-day stake-out of the building down the street where nothing happened. Then I stuffed the bag behind the seat along with the rest of the instant meals and junk I'd collected. *Well, it ain't perfect, but it's better.*

I drove back to the motel. The parking lot was still blocked, so I parked along the far side of the street. I caught sight of Claire as I crossed to the parking lot. Her shoulders dropped, and I couldn't tell if she was relieved or disappointed. Opting for optimism, I strode across the parking lot, passing by a guy who looked like he might be the fire chief.

He spoke into his radio, saying, "Yeah, it looks intentional. You might send an officer out to take a report."

"No shit Sherlock," I muttered as I walked past.

I climbed up to Claire's room, and she ducked inside with me as I crossed the threshold. She was giving me a look that begged, either for information or for a kiss. Since the timing didn't exactly scream "kiss me you fool", I figured she wanted info.

"Ran into a chick at the bar," I said.

Claire rolled her eyes. On her, it was attractive.

"Same one who kicked my ass last night."

"Do tell," she said, smirking.

"She gave me this," I said, holding out the business card. Claire accepted it and looked it over. Written on the back was the name Therin. Her smirk deepened and she handed the card back.

"You two hooking up?"

"No, but apparently she wants us to get in touch."

"Or you at least," she said, the implication so obvious it was an accusation.

"This isn't that."

"Dude, look," she said, holding her hands up I mock surrender, "What you do in your off time is none of my beeswax, but you should know we're never off duty right now."

"She messed with my head somehow. Made me remember-- stuff. I've got to find out what her gift is so we can start making sense of the crap going on down here."

"Ow," she said, "That's tough. What did you do?"

"Nothing, she had me dead to rights," I said, the thought of being waylaid by a street kid, and a girl at that weighing heavy on my mind, "but she didn't kill me like she killed the other guy."

"She killed a man?"

"She killed him right in front of my eyes. Did it with a touch."

"But you she wants to get in touch with?"

"I think she just wants to tell her side of things. She probably thinks I'm a cop or something."

"Max, you <u>are</u> a cop or something."

"Hmph," I said, "Is there anything else you need from here?"

"The cops will want to ask me a few things," she said, "Then we can jet. I don't think they're done with me yet."

I looked out the doorway at the lights that flashed around the walls of the motel. "You called the office yet?"

"Yeah, Toni wants us to come in and debrief. After your incident and now mine, I think she just wants us out of area for a while to let things cool down."

"Shit."

"Tell me about it. I just got a good solid lead on the surveillance footage incident from the hospital parking garage."

"What happened there?"

"An older man was walking to his car, and just as he gets there, he screams like he's in pain and then disappears."

"Were there wavy lines?"

That line earned me a smack on the shoulder and a second look at that real, gorgeous smile. You could say a lot about Claire, she was witty, gutsy and classy, but the best thing about her was that smile.

"No, Doofus," she said, "There was nothing. One minute he was there and then he screamed and he was just gone. There weren't any glitches in the camera footage, and it hasn't been tampered with."

"How'd we get it?"

"The night watchman turned it in to hospital staff, and they sent it to the police. Usually weird stuff either gets ditched there or winds up on the internet before we see it, but this one got passed along. We were especially lucky it didn't wind up in military hands. Nothing personal."

"No problem."

The cops were pulling in as she finished speaking. She excused herself and went down to talk to them. I stood in the doorway as she went down and watched as she flashed her Department of the Interior ID and began her explanation. The officer she was talking to offered up a clipboard, to which she applied a very busy pen and a flourishing signature, handing it back with one of those smiles. *Damn.*

She came back up as the fire trucks were departing, gave me a wink as she whisked past me to retrieve her bags and jacket. I waited for her on the breezeway, and as she came back out, a small riff of wind picked up the wisps of bangs on her forehead. She shivered. The day was getting colder and clouds were rolling in again. I had a feeling it was going to be one of those cold dark Octobers.

THREE

We headed straight for the airport and caught the noon-thirty from Tulsa International to Martin State. There wasn't a lot of travel on Tuesday afternoons, so getting through security was a non-issue. We picked up the tickets Toni had waiting for us at the desk.

I escorted Claire to the terminal gate, and our tickets were checked at the chute. There were only four other passengers on board when we got on. There was a woman with a child, and a set of blond twins in their twenties. I stared at the twins as I squeezed Claire's bag into the overhead. With a bit of absent-minded prodding, it fit--barely. *Where do I know you two from?* An elbow in the side of my leg tore my attention away. Claire evidently thought I was thinking something else.

We took our seats as the rest of the passengers filed on board. Even after boarding was done and the door was closed, the cabin was far from full. Since no one sat behind me and I took the window seat, I sank into the upholstery and then kicked it back as the plane finished its takeoff, and as the engines levelled out, I let them lull me to sleep, and slept off the rest of my hangover as we flew.

When we landed at Martin State Airport, I was surprised to find someone waiting to pick us up. A youngish man with a thin face, piercing blue eyes and a narrow -rimmed version of a fedora held up a sign with both of our last names and the OHP logo. Usually agents had to fend for themselves at the airport. The guy in the hat looked completely thrilled to be here. His scowl reminded me of the scowl on the bartender in Tulsa. It reminded me I still looked like a bum.

The bar. That was where I saw those twins! They'd been the ones singing "Delta Dawn". It was odd that they'd wound up on the same flight as us. I scanned the baggage claim to see if I could spot them, but they were nowhere to be seen. Claire tapped me on the shoulder to indicate that our bags were coming around on the conveyor, and I shambled over to pick them up. Then we went to meet the guy in the hat holding the sign. *Do I know him from somewhere?*

We followed Hat Man to the car. Something didn't sit right. Maybe the twins had me rattled, but the more oddities that piled up the less comfortable I got. It was a company car alright. Right make, model and license plate. The guy had this look in his face, like he thought the whole business of picking up people at the airport was beneath him, and I already didn't like him. He reached for my bag, but I held onto it.

"Actually," I said, "I think I'd rather rent a car."

"Max!" Claire hollered from the front door.

"I have a couple of stops I want to make before we get there." I tried to make my face look apologetic, but I had a feeling it wasn't quite right when the guy's head turned red. "I wouldn't want you to have to sit and wait on me. You want to come, Claire?"

Claire hesitated. She looked unsure whether to tell me off and get in the car, or to grab her bags and come with me.

The guy had her by the arm in an instant. The gun he pressed into her ribcage was a teeny little .38 snub-nose. All but impossible to see, concealed as it had been in his suit.

Hat Man used the elbow he had hold of to keep her off balance. He was trained. She was too, but she didn't dare move much with that gun against her side. I had to do something.

"Get in the car," Hat Man said, sneering.

"Um, no," I said.

"I do not bluff," Hat Man said, pushing the barrel of the little gun harder into her ribcage and giving it a twist, just to make sure she felt it. *Was that a German accent?* Claire winced. It was like barbed wire being pulled through my guts.

"Fine," I said, "Just don't hurt her."

"Get in the car. Driver's seat."

"I'm going," I said. I threw my duffel in the open trunk and opened the rear passenger door. Then I went around and got into the driver's seat. Hat Man ordered Claire to shut the trunk, and then shoved her in the door I'd just opened. He kept the gun on both of us as he opened the front passenger door and locked all of the doors with the push of a button. Then he got in and just held the gun on me.

"You will drive, I will give directions."

"You'll get bent," I said.

The guy must have understood English insults well enough. He knew he'd been insulted. When he popped me in the mouth with the butt of the gun, I saw stars at first. It hurt like hell, but I didn't think he broke any teeth. Licking my swelling, bleeding lip, I put the car in drive. I didn't know what I was going to do now, but I knew that however this all ended, it was going to be supremely painful for Hat Man.

"Turn left out of the driveway and keep going until I tell you."

I did as he directed, and after we drove for the better part of half a mile down the quiet highway, Hat Man told me to take a right at the next road. We turned onto a smaller, shoulderless highway, headed out of town. I either missed the sign or there wasn't one.

The further out we got, the less I liked all of this. We must have gone another thirty minutes through rolling hills. Though the hills were dressed in a Joseph's coat of trees crowned in yellows, russets and reds, it did little to help my mood. I was directed to pull off the highway at a beat-up old mailbox in front of a poorly-hung steel gate.

I turned in and nosed the car up to the gate. Then I put it in park and turned the engine off. I left the keys in the ignition, but made a show of folding my hands and putting them in my lap. He noticed but kept the gun pointed at my head as he levered open the door and backed out. Then he went to the back door to pull Claire out.

In the seconds while he was moving from the front to the back, I was able to slide across the seat and open the door behind him. I saw his eyes widen as he realized too late what I was up to. I stood quickly and caught him with a fist across the jaw before he could even bring his gun around. The guy looked like a bobble-head as he reeled, and I couldn't help but grin as Claire took the opportunity to plant a shoe in his gonads, dropping the guy like a medicine ball.

Claire whooped, and nearly leapt out of the car. She had her hand up, waiting for something like a high five or something. I took a deep breath, and glanced around. No one was watching that I could see, but I just couldn't bring myself to join in her revelry.

"You gonna leave me hanging?"

"Um, yeah," I said, hoping she'd put her hand down and quit acting like a dork.

"Loser."

"Guy's down, your ass is saved. You're welcome."

"Bullshit!" Claire squinted up at me, the blue sky a refreshing change from our usual dark and drear. There were clouds rolling in, but for now it was so bright we were both missing our usual post-sunset hours. "I get half-credit or I'm taking you down next."

"Whatever," I said. I scanned the field beyond the gate, hoping that whatever was beyond the tall grass was Hat Man's boss and that we could get to the bottom of this crazy shit. I bent down and retrieved Hat Man's hat, then relieved him of his coat and gun. "Follow my lead."

Claire marched up the gravel road ahead of me. I had Hat Man's gun pointed at her, as if I was Hat Man and she was my prisoner. She'd rolled her eyes again, but went along with the ruse probably figuring she would pay me back eventually.

When we cleared the gate, I realized that the meandering gravel road curved and then turned down into a shallow depression. It was just deep enough that the tin barn that was there had been hidden from the road. Not that it was a small barn, just that the valley was exactly deep enough. *Perfect place for a hideout.*

When we reached the barn without being stopped or shot at, I felt a flutter in my stomach. *Maybe we'll get out of this alive after all.* Knowing hope for the smiling demon it was, I stepped on its neck and continued as if we were dead already. I tried the door. Not only was it locked, but it didn't budge. It didn't bend, hang loose in its frame, creak or do anything the way an old tin barn door would have.

I banged on the door with my fist. No answer. I banged on the door with the butt of the gun, and then heard a heavy latch slide open inside-- either that or somebody chambered a round in a really big pump action shotgun. Then there was the sound of chains and whining metal-- *gears?*

The whole door, frame and all, seemed to pop inward and then slide on a track. There was a song playing inside. *The House of the Rising Sun.* It was the start of the second verse, and it was playing at a volume I should have been able to hear from outside any ordinary barn. *But then ordinary barns don't have doors with giant latches that ride on tracks with great gears and chains, either.*

Part of me wanted to get the hell out of there, or at least cover our asses, but the rest of me knew that I'd better walk in like I belonged there or Hat Man's buddies would know something was up. I nudged Claire, who was also hesitant, and we took a couple of steps inside. Once we were across the threshold I had to stop and let my eyes adjust, which was just as well, as someone - an older man's voice- hollered for us to stop anyway. The guts knotted in familiar "I'm screwed" fashion and I stood on the spot while my vision slowly returned.

As my surroundings faded into view, I realized that we were standing at the edge of a massive hole in the ground inside the barn. I couldn't see the bottom.

"Oh, I'm so glad you two made it!" The same voice, a little closer now, and to my left. Looking that direction, I saw an old man wagging a lantern quickly in our direction, his long-ass beard flopping perilously close to that lantern as he came. He wore a Hawaiian shirt and khaki shorts with flip-flops and he grinned ear to ear, obviously pleased at the sight of us.

"You didn't hurt Rolf too badly, did you? He was a hard find, and he'll be a good agent once he gets trained up a bit. I apologize for his theatrics. Welcome to the new home of The Office of Human Defense. I'm Arlan, welcome home."

Was that a British accent?

"I'm sorry-- Arlan," I said, lowering the gun but not re-engaging the safety, "You want to tell me just what the fuck that was? The Office doesn't usually resort to kidnapping to get agents home. Especially those who have combat experience. He's lucky it was me. Some of the guys I trained with would have just popped him two, and you'd be putting him in the ground tomorrow."

"Of course," he said, looking a little uncomfortable, "Let's hope you've taught him a lesson. Miss Toni wanted you both to see the new facility before you go back to Oklahoma. It will be spectacular. Come, this way." Arlan led us around the gaping hole on a narrow ledge supported for the moment only by a lattice work of scaffolding which was startlingly lacking in guardrails. OSHA would have a field day, but they would never see this.

"Where is Toni?" Claire asked.

"I'm taking you to her now. She and the director have been in a meeting since seven o'clock this morning. Dr. Pape is also expecting you."

I went ahead and tucked Hat Man's gun into my pocket. I was going to complain to Toni about Hat Man's ineptitude, but once the door opened, every fully-formed thought fell out of my head. Toni walked out of the lantern-lit room, and the warm light backlit her red curls, making them glow. They framed a pale, lightly freckled face that would have been lovely even without the strong jaw and the big green eyes. She would have made any Irish goddess jealous.

I held out a hand, thinking a handshake was in order, but she took it with a familiarity I hadn't expected. We were a long way from downtown, and I wondered if being out in the country had softened her somehow. Fire crept up my neck again, and threatened to engulf my whole face. She must have seen me blush, because she blushed too, and it was-- magic.

I wanted to kiss that hand, but knew better. I was busy contemplating the possibilities when Arlan cleared his throat and we continued in through the little door. No one said anything, but I could feel Claire bristle. Holy shit, was there something there? *Women. Crap.*

FOUR

With my ears burning, I followed Toni into what should have been the tack room, but had been pressed into use as a makeshift office. She stopped short in front of the second laptop along the wall opposite the door and I ran into her. The resultant stoppage brought an exasperated huff from Claire, who was behind me. I fought every single urge I had to say anything, and avoided eye contact with everybody. Arlan cleared his throat again.

The woman seated at the laptop looked up and pulled the old-fashioned glasses off her nose, displacing one dark brown curl from the neat bun it had been tucked into. She smiled up at me, then at Claire. There was a tiny twitch of her right eyebrow while regarding Claire, and then she turned her attention back to me, then to Toni.

"I trust you will enlighten our agents, fresh home from the field, as to the reason behind our brand new fortifications, as well as the findings on the new upshift?"

"Of course, Dr. Pape." Toni led us on around to the back of the room and another computer. There she turned and addressed both Claire and me with complete professional courtesy.

"The Office of Human Protection has received a grant of no small size, and at an incredibly fortunate time." She handed me a file folder and I flipped through it. The folder contained a stack of letters printed out on regular printer paper and signed by hand. They were all addressed to our home office in town. They were addressed to The Office of Human Protection, which most people didn't even know existed, instead of to the Department of the Interior. I glanced over the paper on top, which read:

The Chalice of Flesh
Will be the rebirth of Magic
And the world shall remember
The fear of the dark.

The Council

It was my turn to roll my eyes. "Seriously?"

"Seriously," Toni said as I handed the folder over to Claire. "This 'Council' has sent nineteen letters since 2009. They nearly wound up in the nut-bin file, except that they all went to the same desk, and the person who sat at that desk got a funny feeling about them. Now it looks like this Cabal is actually starting to make things happen."

"Whose desk?" I asked, "It's not like we have a shit-ton of manpower."

"Not important."

"Whose desk?" I pressed her.

"Mine."

I stared at her. How would they even know her? I wanted to vow all kinds of things having to do with blood, but all I could manage at the moment was, "How?"

"We're working on that. We're working on a lot of things," she said, turning to the row of laptops that lined the wall, most of which were empty. It was an odd sight, all those laptops on plastic folding tables along a wall lined with insulation and egg-crate soundproofing. Under the tables, the surge protectors were fed power by extension cords that ran along a dirt floor, probably from some pole I hadn't noticed on the way in. Toni tapped a few keys on the nearest laptop.

"This, she said, huffing red curls out of her face, "Is the frequency of reported anomalous activity in the Tulsa area when I sent you in."

There were only three red dots on the screen, but it was a lot for one town.

"This," she said tapping the key again and then once more, pausing in between for effect, "Is for the last two days."

There were at least thirty red dots after she tapped the button the third time. My stomach lurched. None of us had ever seen a spike like that. Not in a year, much less a couple of days. If we were extremely lucky, we might see that much action in a decade across the whole nation.

"How can this happen?" Claire asked from behind me, "How can it jump like that?"

"Theories abound," Toni said, turning back around to face us and leaning against the table. "The scientists are favoring some kind of electromagnetic resonance to do with some alignment, or some sort of contagion or contamination, but there are other, more esoteric theories as well. That is part of the reason we're building the new facility." Toni directed us back out the way we'd come in, and we stopped outside the office door.

She was still talking, explaining more about the current situation, but I couldn't help looking down the yawning hole in the earth. The darkness below, beaten back by the halogens at ground level, seemed to stretch into the earth forever. *There could be anything down there.* My heart felt like a moth trapped in a light fixture. I wanted to dwell in that expanse. *To fly or to fall. There's death at the bottom of that hole. The unknown is laid bare before me, and mine for the taking...*

"Max?" Toni had hold of my arm and peered up into my eyes. The concern in those green eyes made everything else vanish.

"Yeah," I said, "It's like ripples."

"Actually we're calling it a wave, but yes. Are you okay?"

"Yeah," I lied, "You were saying about the building?"

"It's going to be pretty much like any other building, but underground. It's been designed to dissipate any negative energies directed at it."

"Negative energies?"

"I didn't want to say black magic. We're really just getting started on it. It'll be thirteen stories, and the entrance will be on the bottom."

I had to stifle a pretty stout laugh. "Are you serious? Magic? Like Harry Potter shit?"

"More like X-men shit right now," Toni said, "But yes, it's possible at some point things might get a little 'Harry Potter'."

"At some point. This is already sounding a little Hogwarts to me. Talk to me about the types of activity. Is it pretty much the same stuff, like the psi-anomalies and vortices?"

She shook her head. I'd never seen her eyes so wide. "There have been some reports that have gone right off the charts of weird. And one such report yielded a surprising find."

I shrugged the question. Toni marched over to a gray steel cabinet near the barn's front doors and hauled it open. From the darkness inside she brought out a jar containing yellowy brine and some sort of bug. A big damn bug.

She turned it so the light shone through the foul-looking liquid. The thing had six legs like any other bug, but its head was surprisingly un-bug-like. Two very human looking eyes stared into eternity through the murk. Around them, a shock of black hair sprouted from an oddly mammalian cranium with pointed, chitinous earlobes. From a wickedly broad grin emerged the alien looking sideways mandibles of a stag beetle. It was dead. I shuddered anyway.

I looked over at Claire, but she'd already turned away. Toni put the jar back into the cabinet and turned back to face us as Dr. Pape emerged from the little room followed by a greasy-looking-used-car-salesman type I knew to be Gil Chamberlain. The weasel tagged along just like he was invited, glaring at me.

Claire was still pale as she asked "What the hell could have done that?"

"We think," Dr. Pape answered as she approached, "that the wave or whatever it is unzips the DNA of whatever is in its path and recombines it. But really, that's just a hypothesis. For instance, if this was an ordinary beetle and just happened to be in contact with a person at the time the wave hit it-- that might partially explain this. Still, these kinds of mutations shouldn't be possible. This creature should have died, having been genetically jumbled like that, but it was alive and causing havoc at the zoo."

"Good grief," Claire said.

"That's not even the worst of it. The zookeeper it was touching when it transformed was much more hideous. And he got the wings."

"And what happened to the zookeeper?" Claire's face was ashen.

"He's in containment." It was Toni who answered after garnering a nod of approval from Dr. Pape. "That's another reason for building the updated facility. Also, The Office has a newly-acquired below-top-secret status, so the public will likely know who we are soon. The security has got to be top-notch."

"You called it a wave," I said to Dr. Pape. "Why?"

"Because it seems to expand mostly in one direction, as if something was impeding it on the other side. Right now most of the expansion seems to be from east to west, and its spread broadens north and south as it goes. Like a tidal wave coming into shore. We have no idea what will happen when it completes its lap around the planet. If it stops, all may be well, but if not..."

"All life on Earth will slowly be transformed," It was Arlan who filled in the blank, as he appeared out of the relative darkness to stand beside me. "At least that is the current scientific theory. A more esoteric position might allow for an instantaneous mass-transformation-- A cataclysmic genetic recombination of global proportions."

"But if it happened at a zoo..." I said, rubbing the side of my still aching head, "Was everything there changed?"

"No," Toni said. "We aren't sure why, but not everything the wave impacts seems to be affected." Behind her, Greasy Gil was too busy checking out her ass to glare at me over her shoulder. *I've got to remember to deck that guy.*

"Okay," I said, "So why Oklahoma?"

"That's one of the biggest questions right now," Dr. Pape said, adjusting the collar on her suit. "Speculation is centered on its central location and its relative lag time with societal change."

"Come again?"

"They're last to get the news about anything. It's better now with the internet, but Oklahoma's still a little out of the loop when it comes to what's 'in' with the general populace. That and the large amount of relatively rural area makes it prime real estate for everything from moonshine stills to meth production."

"Not to mention maniacal magic...apparently." I said, "Where do we start?"

"I would start at the sites you two were onto," Toni said, watching me roll my eyes, "Max, you're the metro bars, and Claire you are the hospitals and local news agencies. Follow up on any leads you already have and let's see what the 'in' crowd knows about what's going on. Use better hotels this time, and you might think about changing your appearance. If these guys are on to you, it won't be easy to put one over on them. Work on attire, vehicle choice, hair color and length, and Max, you might even work in SFX makeup-- just to be on the safe side."

"Toni," I said, leaning in just a bit to make her uncomfortable, "There anything else you want to tell me?"

"Yes, but not in mixed company. Max, you and Claire have a job to do. I trust you know it's no more than that."

"Of course." I felt that familiar burn in my face, spun on my heel and walked out the door, leaving Claire standing there gawping.

If this was the new facility, I was going to commandeer a car to take us back to the airport, and it wasn't going to be an old Ford truck. I walked around to the back of the barn and saw rows of vehicles lined up.

There she is... It was a company car, but there was no telling whose. I got into the royal blue Chevelle SS, retrieved the keys from the visor and started it. Claire caught up with me just as I was putting the car in drive. She hopped in, and I gave in to the urge to rev the engine a couple of times before peeling out down the driveway.

As we left the parking area, I just caught sight of the grease-ball at Pape's side before he was obscured by the billowing dust. He was running after us, shouting something about the car. I couldn't stop grinning. Maybe it was worth the fallout later.

I stopped by the car at the gate where Hat Man was just recovering enough to stand. As we retrieved our bags from the car, I heard the man muttering something I couldn't make out. I slung the duffel strap over my shoulder and went over to the guy, slapping a hand on his shoulder.

"Next time, don't be an ass-hat, Hat Man," I said, and grinned even wider, just to show him there were no hard feelings. I heard Claire stifle a giggle. We repacked our belongings into the new car and took off for the airport. I'd call Toni later and tell her where we left it...maybe.

FIVE

The return trip was uneventful, except for the slight turbulence we had over the Smoky Mountains. Turbulence didn't sit well with me. Mama Vierna would have called it a bad omen. She would have poured salt in her shoes, rolled her eyes up in her head and spat. *Her voodoo doesn't scare me anymore.*

I elbowed Claire as we started our descent over Tulsa International. Her snoring interrupted; she sat up with blinky eyes and looked out the window. She didn't say anything-- just kept staring out the window until we landed.

When I stood up to disembark, I offered her my hand. She looked up at me with tears in those big blue eyes, and then put her hand in mine. I helped her up and then hugged her, patting her gently on the back.

"I can't change what we've just seen and heard," I said, "But I can tell you that if there's anything that can be done to stop it, we will."

"I know that," she said, "But what if we can't?"

"We can't afford to think about that right now." I tried on a sympathetic smile. It felt weird. "Come on, we'll take separate cars, and meet up at the Mariott. No fleabag motels this time, kiddo. We're moving up in the world. They might even have Nat Geo on TV." I stood back and let her go ahead of me while I retrieved her bag from the overhead. *Maybe now she won't think I'm a total douchebag.*

She stopped at the end of the chute and I handed her bag to her, then we separated. She rented from Avis, and I rented from Thrifty. I followed her to the hotel, but kept a respectable distance.

She had just checked in and was heading for the elevators when I got to the front desk. I paid for my room and took the next elevator up. When I opened the door to my room, I dropped my duffel and kicked off my Doc Martens, scooting one of the shoes over to hold the door open so Claire could enter discretely.

In the meantime, I moved my duffel bag to the couch so it wouldn't get tripped over, started the little coffee maker and snagged the menu and wine list off the counter. *This is much, much better.* I called down to room service and ordered up burgers and fries with sweet tea since we hadn't eaten all day, and then selected the Gnarly Head Cabernet Sauvignon and two glasses. I hung up feeling vindicated, and actually looking forward to the evening. *Toasted Head is good and if this is anything like that, I'll like it. Plus, anything with Gnarly in the name has to be okay.*

She arrived before the food and wine. She left her shoes at the door and occupied the bathroom to freshen up. When the guy showed up with dinner, all he saw were her shoes. I redirected his wandering eyes with a twenty dollar tip, and he bowed graciously out the door without a word.

A smarter guy might have gone down to the restaurant and brought it up himself.

Claire emerged from the bathroom transformed. She'd let her hair down, and the effect was stunning. Her eyes glittered with mischief when she saw the wine and glasses.

"Maxwell Edison," she grinned, "Are you trying to get me drunk?"

"Yes." I was trying for busted-school-kid face, but I couldn't hold it and had to smile, "Nah, I just thought it'd be good to relax with. We've got legwork in the morning."

"Well that <u>is</u> nice."

Damn that devilish grin. What exactly does <u>she</u> have in mind?

I set the bottle and glasses on the coffee table and picked up my bag to go throw it on the bed, out of the way. When I came back, Claire had taken a seat on the couch and was looking at an old Polaroid instant photo. A very young me looked out of the picture. I was standing in front of a large plantation house, beside an old black woman in a white head-wrap and dress. She had a hand on my shoulder and I looked like I might just be ready to kill the photographer. As I remembered, I was. I hated pictures. Still do.

"Who's this?" Claire asked, still staring at the photo, even as she was handing it to me.

"That's Mama Vierna," I said, laying the picture on the table next to the dinner tray. I went over to the counter to get the corkscrew and when I returned, she was still staring at it. "She raised me. She's my godmother."

"Your godmother? Where are your parents?"

"Missing, presumed dead."

"I can't quit looking at her. She's amazing."

I pulled the cork and poured the glasses. As I did, I studied Claire, studying the picture. I went around the table and sat beside her, setting her glass on the table in front of her, temporarily blocking her view of the photo. She looked at me as if she'd been in a deep daydream. I poured my glass and set it down too, then snagged a couple of fries as well.

"It happens. Mama Vierna has that effect on people. She always had a very commanding presence. Uncle Pat, her boyfriend, liked to say 'she fills up a room'."

"I'm sorry, Max. I never knew. She is striking. Was she very strict?"

"Only when I was real stubborn," I said, leaning back into the couch. "The rest of the time she was just-- family."

That thought birthed a chuckle from somewhere I hadn't felt in a long time, and made me ask her, "How many white boys you know can say they were raised by a Voodoo Queen?"

"It must have been interesting," she said, finally picking a French fry off the tray and nibbling on it absently.

"Never a dull moment. I would have taken a lot more shit about it if she hadn't home-schooled me until I was twelve. And if she wasn't well feared by the locals. Lots of quiet time though. I learned everything you'd ever want to know about rolling candles and making up gris-gris."

"You did voodoo?"

"Not really. I mostly just gathered stuff and helped put stuff together. She was the one who-do-da-voodoo." I took a long sip of the sweet tea and left the wine to breathe.

"But we're not here to talk about my childhood. There's shit going on that needs dealt with, sooner rather than later. One of those things is a skinny red-headed chick that killed a man-mountain and then somehow lost me and still tailed us back to your motel room. The other (not necessarily separate) is who blew up your car. Then there's that thing you were going to follow up on, and this whole wave thing."

"You think they're the same people?"

"Can you not?"

"Most people would say coincidence isn't as rare as we once thought," she said. "And if everything is tied together somehow, then all we have to do is figure out which strands we need to pull for the whole scarf to unravel."

"If this thing is worldwide like Toni was saying, unraveling it might not be as simple as all that. Even if this magic is real magic, it would take Godlike power. No single practitioner has ever had anything like that kind of mojo. Not if it's anything like what Vierna was into."

"We'll just have to dig in and find out what kind of a thing it is," she said, munching down a couple more fries. "It'll all work out. We're the ones who will make sure it does."

"Hell yeah," I said, raising a wine glass which she saluted and then drank to. I took a sip of wine as well. "You said you'd just got a lead on your disappearing man?"

"Yeah, I'm going to see if I can meet up with him in the morning."

"And I'll follow up with Therin. Then we'll see if we can start putting pieces together."

I pulled the now-wrinkled card out of my jeans pocket and flipped it over to read the front. It was a business card for a steel shop out on 97 highway, north of Sapulpa. *I can start here. If she works here, there might be other ties.*

SIX

I woke to a semi-pleasant thrumming on my chest. I reached up a hand to caress what lay there. It was my phone. I swiped the screen and squinted at it to try and see who was calling. My eyes were still too bleary, so I just tapped the green rectangle.

Claire's voice came out of the tiny box. It seemed to be accompanied by the soft cooing sounds hoot owls use to talk to their mates.

"You up or are you gonna sleep all day?"

"Yup," I lied. Sleep hung thick around me, and it was hard to understand what she was saying. I rolled over and fished on the bedside table for the remote, then clicked the TV on. "I'm up and ready for my morning Bloody Mary. You?"

"Shoot, I'm already halfway to the disappearing man's house. You're running behind, mister."

"No I'm not," I said, grumbling the words, "Some of us don't get to crash at nine-thirty and wake up bright-eyed and bushytailed. I've got to keep up with the local night life, remember? Hang on." My eyes having cleared somewhat through vigorous rubbing, I switched the TV channel to the local news.

The reporter on the screen was talking hurriedly about two separate homicides having occurred the night before. "One man died in a car bombing, she said, "And the other was found beaten to death in the back of a strip-mall across town near 91st and Lewis. The authorities are not yet sure if the deaths were related."

The news didn't show any pictures of the victims, but they did show a photo of a man wanted for questioning in the case. It was the man-mountain. They listed his name as Herman Salazar, and said he had been missing since the night before last. Apparently when he didn't return to his job at the Cain's Ballroom, his employers were unable to locate him and called the authorities.

"Be careful," I told her, "I'm going to call Toni. I think our other two agents got killed last night."

"Shit. Okay, bye."

I hung up with Claire and called Toni. She answered with her usual brusque tone.

"Max. Tell me."

"Two dead guys from last night. Are they ours?"

"I haven't heard from Shane or Eric yet. I'll look into it. If agents are being targeted, we have to be extra careful. It means at least one of you has been made. Tell Claire to take steps with her identity as well. I'll let you know more as I find out."

"Sure thing."

I hung up again and called Claire back. The phone tag was already wearing thin. Claire didn't answer. *Maybe she's interviewing the dude's wife already. Maybe not.* I texted her.

"Toni says take ID steps now," I tapped into the little box at the top of the screen. Then as the knot in my guts twisted just a little tighter, I tapped in, "Call me. Important."

I unzipped my duffel and retrieved my shoulder-holster and sidearm, clothes for the day and shower kit. Then I pulled out the box of hair dye and made for the bathroom. I wondered if it might not be better to save that for later, after I finished pissing people off. *I might as well do it. There are other ways of making myself look different.*

I gawked at my reflection in the bathroom mirror. *The scruff has to go.* After I shaved, I mixed up the hair stuff and put it on, wrapping the hotel hand towel around my neck to watch TV while I waited my fifteen minutes.

I picked up the phone off the counter and stared at the screen instead. *Why hasn't she responded?* The minutes crawled by like years, and when the time was finally up, I climbed in the shower but put the phone on the toilet tank where I could reach it if it rang while I was washing up.

I stood there a minute, letting the hot water work its magic on my aching muscles, and ease the creeping pain in my joints. A dull pain pulsed in my chest. The scar tissue inside must have got a jolt last night in the scuffle. *It's never hurt this much before.*

I rinsed the gunk out of my hair and washed it as per instructions, then snagged the towel of the rack and stepped out. When I wiped the steam off the mirror, a near stranger stared back. My hair was a dark ash blond, and I was clean shaven. I combed it and slicked it with some gel and tied it back into a neat curling tail. This should help throw them off.

I had just opened the bathroom door when the phone rang. As I had the phone delicately balanced on top of the pile of clothes and my shower kit, I had to run to the bed to put everything down. I swiped the screen and answered.

"Hey."

"Hey," she said. "What's going on?"

"You might want to head back here as soon as possible. Those two dead guys might actually be ours. Toni's checking, but we really need to do some ID concealment."

"And you?"

"I'm still here. Just getting ready to call on this Therin chick."

"Alright, I'll..." She was cut off. The phone clattered to the ground. There was shuffling and grunting coming from wherever she was. The sound made every part of me tense. My heart beat against its cage. The phone was picked up and a man's voice spoke in her place.

"If you don't want this young woman to meet the same sticky end as your other agents, you'll meet me at the Cain's Ballroom tonight. I'll be out back, wearing a white hat. Oh, and don't bother with all the dramatics, it's just a conversation. I'll even bring your friend."

The guy hung up before I had a chance to tell him how dead he was. I had a location, and an approximate time. They probably didn't know my name, but they knew I was talking to her on the phone. They might not even know that it was me she was talking to, but that was unlikely. They probably at least knew we were partners, and it was probably a trap. *I'm coming anyway, Claire.*

I got my shit together and hauled my ass and my duffel downstairs to the rent-a-car. A gray wind howled around the little car as I made my way toward Sapulpa, making it difficult to keep in my lane going over the bridges and overpasses out of town. The clouds were darkest on the western horizon, and as I headed west I had to turn the headlights on to make sure people could see the little gray car.

Traffic on I-244 was backed up as usual, so I hopped off on I-75 south and went into Sapulpa that way. From there I turned west on 117 and took that all the way to Main. Then it was a straight shot up Main to where it turned into Highway 97. The place I was looking for was on down the road from there, where 97 intersects with 166. Alloy Welding Supply.

Rain erupted from the sky as I turned into the parking lot. By the time I shut off the engine, it was hailing. Thunder boomed around me with a startling intensity. The hail got bigger. *Fuck this.*

I got out of the car, yanking my duffel out behind me and using it as an overhead shield. I beat feet for the door, and slammed into it before I remembered I had to let go of the duffel to open it. I flung the door open, and pulled it quickly closed behind me.

I had just closed it when I heard a sound like a plane coming down fast. This is crazy shit. I dropped the bag and stared out the window. I could feel people coming up behind me, but what was coming out of the sky wasn't a plane. It was a fireball. It looked like it was headed right for us. The noise grew to rock concert levels as the thing approached. I turned to run for distance, only to find my path blocked by three guys in blue striped uniform shirts, who met my eyes with their own wide stares.

"Y'all get down!"

They turned to run too, but as we all took our first steps, the ground didn't seem to be where it was supposed to be and we all found ourselves on the concrete floor. Hard. Unable to recover from the impact, all I could do was roll over and cover my head. The two front windows exploded and I shut my eyes against the flying glass. When the commotion stopped and I could open them, I was surprised to see that the steel door and front wall survived with merely a shudder and a strange bending in. *I wonder if it'll open.*

"What the Sam-Hill-Davis was that? Are you okay, son?"

"Um, sure," I said. I rolled back onto my bruised knees and hands, then gritted my teeth to stand, but it didn't feel like anything was broken. I looked up to see this guy who was maybe mid-to late forties, with a long salt and pepper beard and moustache. I instantly dubbed him DD for Duck Dynasty guy.

"I was just looking for Therin," I said, turning my back on him to go look out the window.

"Who?"

"Therin," I said, staring out through the frame, which hung jagged with tiny shards of glass. "Is she working here today?"

"We don't tell people that sort of stuff," he said quietly, stepping up to stand beside me and gazing at the destruction out front, "Anyway, ain't no Therin working here. Who did you say you were?"

I didn't respond. We just stood there a moment, looking at the crater where my rental used to be. *It's beginning to feel like someone's really got it in for me.* The storm was over and the sky was brightening up. One of the people in the crowd that was gathering to gawk at the new hole in the ground was Therin. I snagged my duffel from beside the door and tried it. It opened. I walked out, leaving DD whispering quiet euphemisms for real obscenities.

She looked up and saw me coming, but after looking, couldn't decide whether to run or not before I reached her.

"What did you do to my car?" We both looked down into the gaping hole where the steam obscured what I was sure was a fairly good sized meteor and the remains of my car.

"Nothing," she said, "I can't do stuff like that, I don't work that way. You shouldn't be here."

"Clearly someone thinks so. And you sent for me, remember? You can't jack into a guy's brain, blow up a car in front of his Motel room, then follow him from said room to his hangout, leave him a card, and not expect him to show up. You must be new at this. Talk about mixed signals."

"I am new at this. Can we please talk somewhere else, though? My lunch is in thirty."

"Fine." I read her facial expressions the whole time she was talking, and she seemed to be straight forward. "How about the Mexican place back down the road? I'll wait there. I'm not hanging around here 'til I start growing green shit anyway. If you don't show, I will find you."

"I will."

I called Toni on my way down the road.

"Max. Are you alright?"

"I'm fine. You?"

"We're alright. The meteor strikes are all over the news."

"Strikes. Plural?" *Good to know it's not personal.*

"All over. Fortunately they're all pretty small. It started on the West coast about an hour ago. It hasn't gotten here yet. They think it might have petered out across the plains. Lots of havoc, but not a lot of casualties so far. If this is tied to whatever is happening, it's bigger than we ever imagined."

"I don't believe in coincidences."

"Max, just be careful."

"That's not going to be possible," I said, the heat returning as I thought of why. "They've got Claire. I've got to go meet some guy at the Cain's."

"Oh, God. I'm sending backup."

"No, I don't want anyone else in the middle of this shit."

"Did I ask you permission? Where are you staying?"

"The Mariott."

"I'll try to have people there this afternoon," she said, "Just don't do anything stupid."

"Whatever." I hung up. *I'm not just letting Claire die on my watch. How can she be so cold about it?* I felt my molars grind, and quickened my stride.

SEVEN

I walked into the little restaurant and chose a corner booth. When the waiter came around, I ordered coffee and stared out at the street through the slats of the red mini blinds. It had started raining again, and this time the rain brought with it a deep chill. The waiter had just returned with my coffee when Therin joined me.

She scurried in the door and straight over to the booth. I hadn't even noticed that I'd been the only customer. She was damp and shivering, her face was flushed and she bit her lip.

"I don't work for anybody," she blurted as her knee began bobbing under the ad-decoupaged table.

"So what was that last night in the alley?"

"You the cops?"

"More like the feds. You want to tell me, or do I keep poking until I find out? The folks in my organization make it their business to find out about creepy shit like that."

"That's what I'm afraid of. That and you won't believe me."

"Again, creepy shit-- is kind of my area." I could feel a grin stealing across my face and worked to maintain my authority. "Try me."

"It just started happening. That guy was going to use me as leverage to get at my brother. He was a drug dealer."

"The guy was a drug dealer?" I asked, taking a small sip from the coffee to see if it was worth drinking, "Or your brother was a drug dealer?"

"The guy was." Therin stopped bobbing her knee and started shaking her foot. "Danny was working undercover for the cops to keep from going to jail. He used to use, but he quit. When he quit, these guys got him busted. Then the cops gave Danny a deal. He had to work real hard to get the dealers to trust him, but they found out he was a snitch. Anyways, G— that's the guy in the alley, he was going to catch me and use me to lure Danny into a trap. I couldn't let him use me to hurt Danny."

"Sounds pretty tidy," I said. I couldn't tell if she was fidgeting and talking fast because she was high, or nervous, or just naturally hyper.

"It's squeaky. It's the truth."

"You a user? You act like a user."

"I was. A little bit. I couldn't score right now if I wanted to. Which I don't."

I sat back and regarded her while I took another sip of my coffee. The waiter brought another glass of water and a menu back around, and Therin gave me that wide-eyed-starving-kid look. I nodded to let her know I'd pay. She ordered the Mucho Gusto Combo platter. *Where the hell is she going to put it all?*

"What's your full name, Therin?"

Therin Jayne Michaels," she said, "And Danny's Daniel James Caldwell. That G guy, he worked for somebody, though. Is this a drug sting?"

Her breakfast arrived before I could answer, so I waited for the waiter to leave before I answered. "No. I don't work for the ATF."

"Oh," she said around a mouthful of juevos y patatas fritas. "Is it like the NSA or something? Are these guys terrorists? Or maybe you're CIA-- are you CIA?"

"No." I set my coffee cup down firmly for emphasis. "Look, Im not here to be interrogated, you are. And besides, I bought you breakfast, so give."

"Sorry. Hey, are they hiring at your job? 'Cause I could totally do that."

"I think you have to have some skills and training."

"I followed you," she said stuffing another mouthful of eggs in.

"I saw you."

"You only saw me because I wanted you to see me. How else was I going to get in touch with you-- telepathy? It's not like you're on Facebook."

"Don't be a smartass."

"Why not? You are."

"...and that is why you can't work at my job. Only room for one. You said this touch thing just started? How does it work?"

Therin scraped up the last of her eggs and taters and washed them down with some of the water. She pushed back her plate and sighed, answering, "I'm not real sure yet. When it first started, it just seemed to make people too scared to do anything to me. It also used to only happen when I was scared."

"Do you remember where you were when it started?"

"Yeah. I was on campus, and some high-school drama queen starts screaming something about me and her boyfriend, then she took a swing. I blacked her eye and thought it was over, but I didn't see the boyfriend come up behind me. He tackled me down and started wailing on me. Broke my nose, see?"

She put a finger on the end of her nose and wiggled it just enough I could hear the cartilage crackle. She continued, "Dude hit really hard, and I was really getting scared he was going to kill me. That's when it happened. He stopped hitting me to choke me, and I grabbed the sides of his face. He jerked backwards so hard he hit his head on the car behind him. Then he just sat there staring into space. He didn't <u>die</u> though."

"So he was fine, but you didn't know what happened. Then what?"

"Then nothing. I went back to living my life. Then there was last night."

"You sure got proficient between then and now," I said, draining the last of the cooling coffee out of my cup. "That doesn't happen without practice."

"Oh sure I practiced. But just with the inside feeling at first, learning how to turn it off and on. Then I got Danny to volunteer for a few days. He was the one who told me what was happening on the receiving end. He said it made him relive the worst moments of his life, sometimes one at a time, and sometimes all at once."

She sucked down the rest of her water in a couple of deep gulps, setting the glass just at the edge of her reach by the wall. "Once I got really carried away and he said I took his worst fears and amplified them. He blacked out completely that time, and scared me to death. He said he was so scared he couldn't think straight. I haven't done it since then until last night."

"Sounds about right."

"I really am sorry. I didn't know who the hell you were."

"I'm just glad you decided not to kill me. Have you ever done anything else with it? Is this fear-casting the only thing?"

"Seems to be."

"Okay," I said, motioning for the check, "can I get a number to reach you?"

"Sure," she said. "Until Danny finds out I'm talking to the Feds."

"He doesn't need to know," I said, taking the pen and folder from the waiter as he brought them over. I slid a twenty in the folder and handed her the pen. "I'm just a friend, and besides, I'm not after you guys anyway, I don't think. I have to go. Somebody I know has been taken and I have to find her. I'll call if I think of anything else."

I tossed a five dollar tip on the table and walked away, leaving the folder on the table as well.

"How do I reach you?" she called after me.

"ESP me," I said as I walked out the door. I walked along the outside wall and looked back in the window. Therin was getting up to leave. As she walked away from the table, I could see that the folder and the five were still exactly where I'd left them on the table. *Maybe she really is an okay kid after all.* I pulled the phone out of my pocket and swiped the screen. I was going to need a new rental.

EIGHT

The phone rang again at just about seven PM as I pulled into the Cain's Ballroom parking lot. A local band was playing tonight, but I didn't care to look at the sign. I checked out all the people and vehicles in the lot. There was no man in a white hat. I thought about Hat Man from the other day and wondered if one asshole might be related to the other.

The call was from Claire's phone. I swiped it and put the thing up to my ear.

"Max?"

"I'm here, Claire. I'm coming to get you, hang tight."

"They're..."

"You hear she's intact. That's all you need to know for now. Come on inside, and let's try not to have any more blood spilled today. Come to the bar and order a Bellywagon. They'll show you where to go."

"Fine, but you put her on the line until I get there. If she's hurt, if you kill her, I'll have my people rain holy hell on this place until they flush you out for me."

"Max?" It was Claire's voice again.

"Hey," I said, pushing through the doors to the bar, "Have they hurt you?"

"Nothing I can't handle." She lied. I could hear it in her voice. "The man in the white hat. I've seen him before, Max. They intend to--"

"Shh. I know. They don't know what they've stepped in. Hang on." I walked up to the bar and leaned over so the bartender could hear me and said, "I'll have a Bellywagon and be quick about it."

The bartender led me around the bar to a little door that couldn't be seen from the front. She gave me a long, sorrowful look as I went in. I put the phone back up to my ear. The hallway was so narrow I almost had to turn sideways for my shoulders to fit. "You still there?"

"Yes, it's still me."

"And you're okay?"

"Yes, I'm-- alright." Something in her voice had changed. It seemed—quieter, and wavered a little.

"I'm almost there." I broke into a run and drew my sidearm as I neared the door at the end. I burst in, ready to duck or shoot as the situation dictated. I immediately drew a bead on the man behind the enormous black desk.

The man there was elderly, skeletal-looking, and was indeed wearing a white western hat. Beside him and also behind the desk, restrained and bruised, sat Claire. She was bleeding from a cut on her face. Her long braid lay on the desk before them, and she now had only short, uneven locks on her head. She'd been crying, and now her tears started again.

I heard the goons slip up beside me, but paid them no mind. All of my focus was on Claire, and that bastard in the chair beside her. Their guns clicked and clattered to let me know they were ready for shooting. Blood thrummed through me, and I could feel my jaw clamp down on the bile rising in my gullet. *Wait your turns, boys. I'll get to you in just a minute.*

"Please Mr. Edison, sit." The man behind the desk smiled serenely as he said, "we're all gentlemen here. Well, except for the whore."

"Gentlemen don't call women whores," I managed to growl through my teeth. "They don't beat on 'em either."

"Ah, I see you are still under the impression that she's on your side." The man stood on his stick legs and walked around her chair, laying one bony hand on her shorn hair. "Nothing could be further from the truth, you know."

"I haven't really picked a side yet, so how do you know? What are the sides, so I can make an informed choice?"

"Because," he continued as if I hadn't spoken at all, "I hired her to help take down your organization from the inside. It's a little embarrassing, don't you think?"

"I'll be leaving, if it's all the same, and I'll take Claire now."

There was pain. Light exploded behind my eyes and then all was darkness. When I came back around, I was sitting in a chair. Well, I was duct-taped to a chair, and my .45 was gone. Claire was still on the other side of the desk, but the man in the hat was now sitting genteelly on the corner of the desk, watching me with his head cocked to one side. The word reptilian sprang to mind.

"What the hell do you want?"

"Your cooperation would be nice for a start, though in the end your actions will be irrelevant. I am Reginald Arcturis Hurt the third. I represent a collective of dissenting voices in the world, but more specifically in the United States. There must be a change in the world, my boy, a deep and drastic change. We are the ones who will institute that change.
Your 'Office of Human Protection' would have us stopped if it were possible. Surely you see how futile such an effort would be?

It really is embarrassing; all of you running around chasing Bigfoot when there are real terrors. Man is the real terror on this planet. Surely you've noticed."

"So you're just the voice of reason in a world gone mad, huh?"

"<u>A</u> voice, naturally. Just think, if humans were truly one with their world, how much better we would treat it. If we would bring humanity back to a state in which we were natural creatures again, magic would blossom back into the world and these governments and corporations like mine would cease to rule. Magic would rule instead."

"You're out of your mind. Magic? Dude, come on. Even wiccans don't really believe in that shit."

"Oh, but they do. And with good reason. Coming days will prove just how right they were. And you'll want to be on the right side when it happens."

"When what happens? You still haven't told me anything about whose side I'm supposed to be on."

"The winning side, of course. We have work in progress that will shake the very fabric of reality. Magic <u>will</u> be birthed back into the world, and man will be transformed."

"We'll stop you."

"I'm afraid that's impossible. Events are already in motion to prevent government interference. The work is already nearly complete. You see, we've been working at this for years already. The fact that you are just catching on is a testament to the abilities of <u>my</u> organization. The Office of Human Protection has only moments left in existence. This Society only days. Come work for me, and spare yourself the fate of your coworkers."

"What are you going to do?"

"Watch," he said. He said it grinning, with the wistful air of an entertainer who was about to put on a hell of a show. Hurt then picked up a remote and clicked it at a point somewhere behind me. Then he motioned to one of his goons, who turned my chair around to face an enormous television screen that was revealed as a section of the wall folded away.

On the screen was a dirt road that led through a familiar-looking rust-red gate to an old barn with a rust-red roof to match. I recognized the construction site for the new office building just as Hurt pressed another button. When he did, the barn exploded with such force it created a mushroom cloud.

I felt like my guts were going to come out my mouth. I bit down on my teeth to keep from crying out, but I couldn't help thinking about Toni. *Toni was in there the other day. Was she in there just now? What about Dr. Pape and that weird Hawaiian shirt guy-- Arlan? How many others?*

The goon turned my chair back around again and Hurt returned to his seat beside Claire on the other side of the desk. I didn't want to look at her, but the motion of her eyes drooping caught my attention. Though she tried to keep it from showing, her head nodded. She didn't look good. *I wish you could tell me what you're feeling. Why couldn't you be telepathic like Therin?*

"The question is, Mr. Edison, what will you do?"

I clenched my jaw even harder and strained against the duct tape. I knew if I said anything, it would likely just get us both killed. So I just glared at him.

Hurt continued with a satisfied grin on that flesh-coated skull, "What you will do now is you will return to see if anyone survives in your organization, and you will finish your so-called investigations. If anyone questions you further, you will tell them that nothing detrimental to mankind is going on here in Oklahoma. That's the truth. We are working to save mankind from itself, from the unmaintainable status quo. Just tell them the truth."

"What happens to Claire?" I was finally able to ask.

"Claire is a traitor to the United States of America, humanity, and the all the plant and animal kingdoms. She will die. Actually, she already has."

I followed Hurt's gaze back to Claire, and found her slumped forward against the tape that held her securely to the chair. I couldn't tell if she was breathing or not.

At a gesture from Hurt, the two goons went over and lifted Claire's chair up and carried her toward the door. That's when I noticed the blood that had been running down her leg. It dripped off her bare foot as they carried her around the desk. One of them looked up, and though the pounding in my chest was making it hurt again, I couldn't help noticing his face. It was the face of the guy from the alley. Somehow my heart pounded even harder.

I looked down at my own feet, to find they were in a pool of viscous red liquid which was crusting around my shoes. I did a mental check, and did not feel any cuts on my body anywhere. It must have been Claire's blood. *They severed her femoral artery. She bled out with me sitting right here! Even if I'd known, she'd have died too fast to stop it.*

I waited for the goons to leave, then twisted in the tape, rocking back and forth in the chair to try and get it to tip. Still grinning, Hurt came around and placed those bony hands on my arms, applying just enough pressure to keep the chair from rocking. He grinned into my face.

"Please, don't trouble yourself. You'll be free to go in just a moment. There will be an inquiry. All you have to do is tell the truth. We wouldn't want any more deaths than absolutely necessary."

I tried to head-butt him and crack that bony skull, but he straightened up just in time for me to miss. He let go, and the momentum of the move was just enough to land me on my face. I was still tied to the chair, so my weight was all on my face, neck and upper chest. My chest was beginning to hurt so bad it was getting hard to breathe. *Heart attack?*

At my uncomfortable angle, I could just see Hurt pick up his remote again, brandishing it with a flourishing motion as if it were a magic wand. There was a loud clack, and I was falling again-- falling through a close blackness. Then there was a crashing, a lot of pain, and then nothing. No light, no sound, no pain.

When I woke up, the pain returned—chest pain included. My eyes adjusted to the darkness, and as it cleared up, I could see that I was in a tunnel of some kind. I was still mostly taped to the chair, but it was busted now, so I could move my arms and legs.

I worked at the duct tape around my right arm with my teeth. After gaining a small tear in the tape, I got as good a bite as I could and pulled with my teeth and my other hand, working my way through it. With my newly freed right hand, I fished my pocketknife out and cut away the rest.

When I was free of my chair pieces, I stood up. I pulled my phone out and pressed it into service as a flashlight. It did little to dispel the gloom, but it gave me a few feet more of fair sight. The ceiling of the tunnel was probably two feet above my upstretched arm. *Probably an eight-foot ceiling.* The tunnel was maybe another eight feet wide and there was about a three foot wide trench full of water through the middle.

I spotted something by the water's edge, in among the broken chair pieces, and I stooped to pick it up. As I grabbed hold of it, something about the size of my forearm lunged out of the water at my hand.

I scrambled backward, crab-like, nearly breaking my phone in the process. I watched as more and more of them broke the surface of the water. Their chaotic breaching and writhing made the water look like it was boiling.

Another creature leapt from the water, this one landing less than a foot away from me. This one looked like some sort of wigged-out cross between a barracuda and a flying fish. *I've got to find an exit, ASAP.*

I glanced left and right, but my range of vision was pretty short. There was no way to tell North from South, so I just stood and made my way to my left, keeping as close as possible to the wall. As I moved down the tunnel, I started seeing less of the creatures. Damn things gave me the heebie jeebies.

About fifteen feet down from my original position, I saw what looked like a ladder-- across the water. *Well, shit.* I kept going and eventually came to a ladder on my side, but when I climbed up to shove off the manhole cover, it wouldn't budge. The holes were covered up. Something was sitting on it topside.

I climbed back down and continued down the tunnel. Finally I came to one end of the section I was in, and saw a great arched opening leading to the next section. Unfortunately for me, it was crossed and crisscrossed with rebar which had been embedded into concrete on either side. There was no way out here. I had to go back down the tunnel and try to cross to the other manhole, but I had a feeling it was going to be blocked as well.

I used the time it took to walk back to the other ladder to steel my nerves for the jump. Visions of creatures dragging me down into the sewage plagued my every step. I had just about banished them completely when a gut-deep scream yanked away all the progress I'd made. It was a woman's voice. *Claire.*

That scream echoed off the walls, and was swiftly followed by another one. The second scream peeled off the shock of the first and set my legs in motion. I ran. The thought that she was somehow still alive made me feel like I was flying.

When she came into view, she was trying to crawl out of the roiling red water. She had those things stuck to her. What hair she had left, no longer golden, was plastered to her head. I dropped the phone and the light went out. Almost completely blind, I reached for her and grasped her arms. There was an enormous amount of splashing, which soaked me through when I finally made contact. I groped for her in the darkness, what little light there was finally allowing me to see shifting, writhing blue-black tentacles.

She was slippery, and she grabbed at my jacket with unexpected strength. I pulled, as much to keep from being pulled in as to heave her out of the water, and she screamed again. This time only half a scream, but her face was still frozen in terror. She was lighter than she should have been, and I fell backward with her. With half of her.

When I realized what had happened, I lost it for a minute. Her hands had relaxed and when I shoved her off of me, she slipped back into the water. She didn't sink immediately. The roiling of the water slowed a little, and her terror-stricken face stared back at me in the murk.

I felt a massive pressure on the outside of my ribcage, and I thought I was going to implode from the wrongness of the scene. Just then, something much, much larger coiled around what was left of Claire and pulled her under. The water became still again.

When I was able to move, I found my feet and stood on still-shaking legs. Then I ran for my life.

Fueled by adrenaline, I ran back down the tunnel to where I'd found the other ladder and leapt across without thinking much. *If I'm going to die, I want it to be over quick. I don't want to see Claire's face anymore.*

I hefted the manhole cover off with one shoulder and then used both hands to shove it across and open the hole. I rolled out onto the empty street onto my back and tried to catch my breath and drive the sight of Claire from behind my eyes. Failing at that, I sat up and looked around. All of my worst days ended on a deserted street.

There was a buzzing in my pocket. I'd never got a chance to look at what it was I recovered from the broken chair.

It was Claire's flip-phone and hotel key. They were stuck together with some sort of lanyard thing. It was Toni. I didn't answer. I couldn't. Not yet. I thought about going back to the Cain's but the man and his goons would be long gone. Then I wondered about how far I was from the lounge.

NINE

The cab dropped me off at the hotel and I dragged myself inside and toward the elevator. The sleek, gleaming tile and elegant carpet were enough of a shock to make me self-conscious. As I trudged past the poor old woman at the desk, she cringed at the sight of me. The look she gave me threatened a scream if I came near her. When I turned around to hit the button on the elevator panel, I realized I'd left a trail of blood and mud behind me. I glanced back to the woman at the desk, who whispered frantically into the desk phone.

Go ahead, lady. Call the cops. I've got a few choice words for them. Absently I stuck the key card into the slot and opened the door, only it wasn't my door, and it wasn't my key card. It was Claire's door. Claire's key. Dead Claire's. Dead like the guys in Fallujah. I saw her face again, and realized it was worse. She'd been eaten by monsters-- real, living, physical monsters.

These were the kinds of monsters we were supposed to be protecting humanity from, but they weren't supposed to actually exist. *Not like that. ESP, sure, some random adaptations, fine. This is horseshit. I have to call Toni and see if I still have a job.*

I dropped my duffel and sat on Claire's couch. My eyes got really hot, so I sat and rubbed them for a while, and then I got up and collected her things. Everything that looked like it might belong to her, I shoved into one of the two bags she'd brought. Then I retrieved my duffel and lugged everything to my own room. Dropping my duffel inside the door, I set her bags on my couch, and then proceeded into the bedroom to flop.

Exhausted, sprawling across the still-made bed, I retrieved the phone from my pocket and swiped the bar at the bottom of the screen. I tapped the contacts icon. Three names showed on the screen. One of them was Claire's, another was Toni's. I had to work to steady my hand as I reached up to touch Toni's name.

The phone rang. It rang again. I felt my throat tighten as it rang a third time. I hadn't realized I was holding my breath until it came rushing out when Toni's voice replaced the fourth ring.

"Max." She said, "I can't talk now."

"Claire's dead."

"So are a lot of other people."

"You sent her to me and now she's *dead*!" I hadn't meant to shout it, but I had. My throat wanted to close around the words, take them back, but I wound up clenching my jaw in refusal. When Toni replied, her voice broke.

"Max, they blew it up. They bombed the office site."

"I know. I know who it was, too. The son-of-a-bitch made me watch it blow up while Claire was bleeding out in the same room. She was three feet away from me Toni, and then they fed her to these... creatures in the sewer."

"I'm so sorry, Max. I wish I knew what to say."

"Yeah, I know. Sorry I yelled."

"It's okay. Look, why don't you come back home. It's just too volatile there. We're going to have to re-work everything. They're calling for an official inquiry, and it's not looking good if we can't get a lot more support from DC. We could all be out of a job."

"I can't come in and report yet. They want me to tell you nothing is going on. He told me that Claire was sent to take down The Office from the inside. Then they killed her, presumably for failing."

"Do come in. Just tell them the truth."

A flash of heat seared its way up around my neck and I found myself sitting bolt upright in the bed. "That was what Hurt said. Those exact words."

"Well, what is the truth, Max?

I swallowed the sudden suspicion I'd felt, and forced myself to reply. "That we can't prove anything. Everything we have is circumstantial, and nothing really seems to connect concretely to anything else. We're getting shut down. Too much money and too many lives, and for what?" I could feel my throat closing again, so I swallowed hard and said, "I've got to go."

I hung up before she could argue, and just sat there a minute, letting it all sink in. The monsters in the sewer, Claire, Therin, the truck getting struck by the meteor and the sudden freak storm.

So just who is this guy? Sure, he's rich, and has lots of hired muscle, connections, and who knows what, but the letters said council. Just where does he rank in that outfit, and what kind of bad juju are they into? More importantly, is Hurt right? The thought made my stomach knot like I'd had a bad batch of mussels. *No. Nobody wants someone out of the way just for being embarrassing. This council felt threatened. Whatever this is, it is exactly my business.*

I psyched myself up for the task of going through Claire's things. I went back to the couch, sat down and unzipped the first bag. Inside I found a lot of clothing, a small satchel and an envelope marked: To Rachel.

I knew what it was. I'd sent enough of them. I would drop it in the mail in the morning. No way was I going to defile her last letter to her family. Opening the satchel, I found a stack of files, and her voice recorder. I laid the recorder and the envelope on the table gently. These would have my full attention later. I pulled the files out and put them on the table as well. Then it was on to the other bag.

This bag contained mostly personal items, makeup, feminine supplies, and her civilian billfold and planner. There was also a full-size manila envelope, which had no writing on it, but was sealed with both the regular adhesive and a wax seal. The emblem was hard to make out, having evidently been through some misadventure or other, and I laid this, along with her planner aside as well. If I was going to get to the bottom of Claire's involvement, this seemed like as good a place as any to start.

As I dug a little more in the bottom of the bag, my little finger caught on a loop of some sort. When I tried to pull it out, I heard the distinct crackle of Velcro. My curiosity piqued, I dumped the rest of the stuff out onto the couch and gave the loop a healthy tug.

The false bottom of the purse gave way, revealing that the bag's bottom was papered with ten-thousand-dollar bills. I couldn't tell how many until I pulled them out, so I pulled the stacks out one by one. There must have been hundreds of bills here. Whoever these belonged to would come looking for them, no doubt. *Unless they belonged to Claire...either way, they're evidence I didn't have before.*

Time was growing short until either they or the police showed up, so I stuffed the important stuff in the little satchel and stuffed the satchel in my duffel. Then I locked the door, peeled off my blood-crusted clothes and hit the shower. I washed quickly, and got out and dressed within a few minutes. Still, I knew things were converging and I pushed even harder to get out. I called a cab as I was slipping my shoes back on, and then snagged the two complimentary water bottles and strode out the door. Once safely out of the room, I dialed Therin's number on my cell.

Just as I reached the elevator, I saw the red and blue lights reflecting in flashes off the polished surfaces around the wall trim and railings. *Fuck, I have no time for cops now.* I took the stairs instead, and ducked through the door just as the officers were coming through the entrance.

When I hit the landing for the second floor, I got out of the main stairwell, and took the service elevator down to ground level, coming out between the kitchen and the laundry room. Ducking into the laundry, I stuffed the duffel down into a laundry bin and threw a chef's smock over my clothes..

Hoping like hell nobody would ask why a chef was pushing a laundry cart, I wheeled the cart to the back door, and pushed the bar, taking a deep breath of the crisp air once I was out. Then I pulled my duffel out and ditched the smock in the laundry bin, parking it by the back door. Then, as calmly as I could manage, I walked around to the front of the hotel to meet my cab. No one seemed to notice when I tossed in my duffel and sat down, closing the door gently behind me.

I pushed "send" on the phone. It rang twice before Therin answered.

"Hey Fed."

"Hey. Don't call me Fed. Name's Max. Can you meet me?"

"Sure, where?"

"Super 8 on New Sapulpa Road?"

"On my way, what's up?"

"I need a favor, I'll tell you when you get there. Meet me in the lobby."

"Got it."

I hung up and looked at the driver. "Super 8, Sapulpa."

"Sorry sir, we don't go out that far."

"Alright, Cain's Ballroom, and I'm kind of in a hurry."

"No problem."

We reached the Cain's in about twenty minutes. I was kind of worried Therin would be sitting at the hotel waiting, but I paid the man and went to retrieve my rental car. Interestingly, I met no resistance. I checked the car for explosives, threw in my duffel, then got in and drove like a bat out of hell all the way to the hotel. I got there just in time to see Therin walk in the doors, in her hoodie, light sweater and shredded denim mini skirt with black tights and boots. It was just strange how she made all that weird shit work together. Maybe she could be some help even for an old thirty-something geezer like me.

I grabbed my bag and sprinted for the doors. I was glad I'd taken the time to clean up, so I didn't scare the chick at this counter when I checked in. She handed me a set of key cards for room 308 and then I headed to the lobby to collect Therin. Tapping her on the shoulder, I had to suppress a chuckle when she squeaked as she spun around.

I turned away quickly, so she wouldn't see the grin I couldn't help and led her to the elevator and pushed the button. My grin under control, I got in and then pushed the button after she was safely through the doors. We went to the room, and once inside, I flipped the lock and twitched the front curtain panels closed. Nothing had looked suspicious, but you could never be too sure.

When I turned back to look at Therin, her eyes were too wide, and her face was drawn. I'd scared her.

"Sorry for the cloak and dagger," I said, trying to sound calm and sure of myself. "I got into a bit of a tight spot back there. I can't afford to be held up by the local cops right now, and I can't take the chance that they'll have a leak to the guy that's out to kill my organization. I need to disappear. Can you help me change my look enough to not be recognized?"

"Can I? Hell yes, but why should I?"

"In the name of your country and all that is holy."

"God and country? Not really my thing."

"My partner, Claire? They just murdered her." When her expression didn't soften I knew it would take more than just a death of someone she didn't know. "She died horribly at the hands of these monsters. They fed her to these—creatures, but they're not going to stop at just killing a few people in one lousy organization. They need us out of the way because they've got plans that go worldwide, sister." The heat returned to the back of my neck, and the lump had returned to my throat as well. This shit was for the birds. She needed to be scared. She needed to know what was coming if these bastards weren't stopped.

"They want," I continued, "to do something big, something that will affect the whole world, and they're murderers. They've already killed who knows how many. That explosion in Maryland? That was them. Do you really want to see what they have in mind for the whole planet?" Therin shook her head. Her eyes were wide again. My words had obviously hit their mark.

"No, not particularly. Freakin' terrorists. What have you got to work with?"

I dug out Claire's makeup kit, along with my green contacts and Halloween stuff and spread them out on the desk. Therin turned on all the lights in the room, including the little desk lamp, which she twisted around to where the light fell directly on my face. Then she went to open the drapes on the outside window, but I caught her arm. A simple shake of my head conveyed the message, and she returned to the desk, the drapes still closed. She had me sit in the desk chair, and gave me a good looking-over.

"Did I ever tell you what my major was in college?"

"No," I said, a slight twist of my stomach giving me something to think about.

"I'm a film student," she said grinning, "My specialty is videography, but I loved the theater makeup class. I sideline doing makeup for cosplayers.

"Cosplayers?"

"People who dress up for conventions, kind of like the one that's going on in town this weekend."

"Really? Well, nothing too crazy. The key to infiltration is blending. Klingons don't blend too well."

"Understatement is the key to good makeup," she said. "See? We'll get along fine."

"Okay, no offense," I said, "But I just lost a partner. I'm not in the market for a new one. This is just a favor, got it? Then you go your way and I go mine."

"Dot it..." she said, giving me a mock salute. Then she handed me the green contacts. "Put these in for a start."

I popped the contacts in, and while I was still blinking, she started smearing some of Claire's liquid foundation on my face. Her skin was a lot lighter than mine, so Therin put the makeup all the way down my neck and blended it at the collarbone. Then she put it on my arms and the backs of my hands as well. Suddenly I was really glad it was fall.

There was a flurry of stuff she said that I didn't really comprehend as she smashed some of the Halloween latex on my nose along with the foam goop to round it out a bit, covered that with makeup, and then she was drawing on my eyebrows with some pencil. Next she got the big brushes and powders and started putting them on in layers.

Once she was done, she turned me back around to face the mirror behind the desk. The change was amazing. I couldn't have done anything like that. I looked much thinner in the face. Almost gaunt. I looked older, but kind of distinguished. I almost looked like those old comics of Dr strange, but without the white streaks in my hair. Then she hit me with the bad news.

"It's a difference, but I think they'd still know who you are. If you really want to fool anybody, you've got to do something drastic with your hair. I think you need to let me give you a serious haircut."

"Horseshit! No way."

"It's either that, or I can shave it."

"Where's the clippers?"

TEN

My hair was now short as well as blond. Therin's offhanded comment only served to make me even more self-conscious.

"It's a shame really," she grinned at me, "You were sexier with long hair."

"Stop it," I said, slapping the hair off my shoulders. I went in the bathroom and put on some of the other clothes I brought. Black slacks and a light gray button up shirt. Hoping it would be different enough, I came back out and presented the whole bit for Therin's approval.

She let out a low whistle and said, "It's like Sonny Crockett put on the Mac Daddy."

I rolled my eyes, mocking her earlier expression and snagged my denim jacket off the armchair. Before I got one arm in, Therin yanked it out of my hands. My shock must have been all over my face, because she snorted.

"You can't put that on with those clothes. Go out and get a decent jacket. Something nice. No denim. No leather either. Tweed maybe. Silk's better."

"I don't have time for this shit."

"You need to make time. It's just a few minutes and if you put that jacket on, they're gonna know it's you, dumbass. I thought you did this for a living."

"I do. Hang on," I said. I dug around in the old duffel and came out with the jacket that went with the slacks. While I was at it I grabbed the belt and dress shoes.

"See. Somebody did teach you how to dress once upon a time," she said snapping the lid shut on Claire's overnight, her eyes twinkling.

"Therin, thank you," I said, " This really is great. You might work on a new look for yourself, too. You can take the makeup and stuff with you. I won't need it again."

"How come?"

"After tomorrow I won't be around, and I don't want you to come looking, okay?"

"No." She hefted up the case and stood defiantly between me and the door. "It's not okay. I risked my life to try and help you out. Not once but twice. You owe me, and Daniel and I need your help. These guys aren't just going to leave me alone because I killed G. They're gonna be pissed. What are we supposed to do?"

"You said your brother was working undercover with the police?"

"Yeah."

"So let him. You keep your head down and let him finish his sting. Maybe get out of town for a few days. Go stay with family or something. Keep from being the leverage they need. Tagging along after an agent will get you killed sooner rather than later."

"What are you, scared?"

"Maybe. You definitely should be."

Something in her face softened and I knew. She'd seen it. She needed to leave and now. Maybe she'd touched my mind and picked up on it that way.

"It's not you."

"Therin— stop." My whole head was hot. My eyes felt like they were made of molten steel. I looked everywhere but in her direction and fought to grind this feeling to a halt, but was slipping further every minute she stood there looking up at me with those big eyes. I was not going to turn into a blubbering kid in front of her or anyone else.

"No but really, people die all the time. You didn't kill them."

"You need to go."

"Max..."

"Therin, please."

Her face hardened again, her jaw set.

"Fine, she said. "But don't come crying to me for help again. I'm done."

She slammed the door as she left. She'd left just in time. The first and last of those molten tears popped out and landed on the lapel of my suit jacket. I took a deep breath and turned back to pack up the rest of the stuff when my eyes fell on that envelope and nearly started the whole mess again.

I sat on the end of the bed and looked at the seal. It was a lion, but it looked like it had other heads sticking out of it. It kind of looked like an old photo I'd seen somewhere. I took the notepad and pencil from the nightstand and made a rubbing of the seal in case I destroyed it opening the envelope.

I eased the edge of my pocket knife under the gum on either side and then slid it carefully under the wax seal itself. It popped free unbroken and the envelope was open. I reached in carefully and removed the contents. Within were a picture and what looked to be a set of instructions. The picture was me.

So, Claire had been ordered to kill me, but by whom? She'd never gotten to read the orders, but would she really kill a fellow agent? Had she killed the others? How well did I really know her? We'd just been to the construction site for the new Office. Had she been the one to plant the device? No, of course not. She was with me the whole time.

I dug out her planner next. If I could get an idea of where she was going, maybe I could work out what she was up to. The date she had made for yesterday was with a Mr. Jim Madsen at 4215 South Jamestown. That done, I used my phone to look up Reginald Arcturis Hurt, III. I didn't find the name exactly, but the ornate listing and sleek website screamed Reginald to me. Hurt Global. The picture showed the Hurt Tower dominating the Tulsa skyline. According to the site, its rotating form was driven by the sun, completely independent of the power grid. It was supposedly an advanced technologies company.

Now that I knew where to look for the creepy bastard, I stuffed the rest of the items in my duffel and hauled it out the door with me. Sonofabitch was mine now. He'd have the whole goddamn world if I let him. There was just one more stop to make before I left. I stopped at the liquor store on my way out of town and picked up a fifth of rum. When I got to the counter, the clerk frowned for a moment over the top of her newspaper and then folded it onto the counter, her multitude of bangle bracelets clacking against the Formica.

ELEVEN

The address in Claire's case file about the disappearing man led me to an address just off South Lewis. The little bungalow's front windows were already glowing and a little Scotty dog yipped at me from the fenced-in front yard. A gray-haired woman in a floppy garden hat looked up from weeding her daylilies as I got out of the car. Her sun-wrinkled face formed starbursts at the edges of her eyes when she smiled at me.

"Come on up," she said. "Don't mind Francis, he loves people."

"Mrs. Morris?"

"That's me," she said. She was a classic beauty, if a little on past her prime.

"I'm Max, Maxwell Edison. I'd like to ask you a few questions about your husband Jack."

"Why? What's happened? Has he done something?" Her face had gone from warmly open to hard and waspish in less than a second.

"When's the last time you saw your husband, Mrs. Morris?"

"About thirty minutes ago."

"Do huh?" *Well that fucked up my whole line of questioning.*

"He's just in the kitchen making supper. You want me to go get him?"

"He's here? He's okay?"

"Well of course, why wouldn't he be?" She stood and pulled off her gloves, regarding me with a kind of suspicious condescension.

"Maybe I ought to talk to him then," I said, letting my wide eyes do all the talking, and holding my hands out, palms up.

She gave me a sidelong glance as she turned toward the house. I hadn't said what I wanted or who I was with. I didn't move to follow her. She went in and made sure to close the solid door behind her. Jack came out soon enough. He was definitely the guy from the video. He came down the stairs into the garden and stuck a hand out to me. I took it and returned his grin.

"You gave some folks quite a scare," I said.

"Did I?" he asked.

I leaned in so I could whisper like a kid playing at spy, 'Your little disappearing act in the parking garage the other day. Nice."

"Oh, um..." he looked back toward the door of the house.

"No need to be shy," I said in my most conspiratorial tone, "In fact, I'd like to know what I can do to help."

"You can help?"

"Almost definitely," I said, leaning on the same section of fence his wife had just vacated. "But you have to tell me exactly what happened."

"Well," he said lowering his voice, "my wife doesn't exactly know about it yet, so could we take a walk?"

"Sure."

Jack swept a hand through his silvering hair and made his way to the gate. A couple of gentle words kept the dog, Frances from following Jack out, and he turned back to smile an apology to me. I returned it and we meandered down the driveway past my rental.

"I didn't really know what was happening to me," he said easily enough. "It was like being torn apart from the inside—rearranged somehow. Then it just stopped and I started to get in my car. That was when I saw that I didn't have a reflection. All I could see was my clothes."

I nodded, keeping a slow pace so I didn't leave him behind.

"Well, I couldn't very well be seen like that, could I—no pun intended—so I took off the clothes and put them in the car. I couldn't drive like that, so I decided to walk home. The only problem was that it went away about halfway home. People started yelling at me, and I looked down and realized they could see me. All of me. I ducked down an alley and hid between some dumpsters."

I felt my eyebrow begin to climb up my forehead.

"I only made it because there was some clothes in one of the dumpsters, and even then they was for some real big fella. I had to cinch them up and go back for the car. Hand 'em halfway up to my armpits," he chuckled, "but if I hadn't found 'em I'd be in jail right now, and I think my wife would be a widow...or a divorcee."

"Can you describe the clothes?"

"Big tan flannel shirt and some faded black slacks."

"No sign of the guy they might have fit?"

"No, why?"

"Nothing you need to worry about right now," I said as gently as possible. "Please, go on."

"Well, there's not really anything after that. I just came home and was glad to be here."

"Can you tell me what you were thinking and feeling right before the change?"

"I was kinda upset. I lost my job, see, and at my age, it'll be hard to find anything at all now."

"Where did you work?"

"I was the janitorial supervisor over at Hurt Tower. Been with that asshole since he was a high-school graduate, and this is the thanks I get."

"Were there any other sensations?"

"Well, for a moment it felt like there were these scales or plates on my skin—where did you say you were from?"

"I didn't, but I work for the government. Would you like to see my ID?"

"Nah, you seem all right. I wanted to do that too, when I retired from the air force, but Jamie said that the government wasn't normal anymore, and it was normal or nothin'. Hey, is this some kind of testing thing that went wrong?"

"Nah," I said chuckling, and clapping a hand on his shoulder gently as we walked, "We're not really sure what happened to you. That's why I'm here. Would you be willing to have some tests done to see if we can figure out what's happening to you?"

"Is that why you're here?" He stopped, removing his shoulder from beneath my hand by taking a not-so-subtle step away from me. "You gonna lock me up in one of them camps?"

"Of course not," I said, "We'd just like to help you figure it out so if it happens to someone else, we'll know what it is. Maybe how to help them."

"That doesn't sound so bad." Jack looked straight ahead now, his eyes searching, his jaw set. I could see he wanted to trust me, but was struggling with something I couldn't read. There was no telling what the old guy had seen in his time.

"If you like," I offered, "I'll do it when we get back to the house. I can take the hair, skin and blood samples myself with the kit in the car. That way you never have to leave home, and nobody has to be the wiser."

"I guess we could do that," he said, turning to study my face, "but what do I tell Jamie?"

"You might just say you had a spell the other day after work and they sent me around to make sure you're alright."

"She'd never buy that the company sent you, those bastards don't give a shit about their people. Past or present. I'll say you're from their insurance company, and that they want to make sure they don't get sued. She might give you some dirty looks, but she'll keep her paranoid nose out."

I gave him a level look.

"Oh, I love her, but she's one of them tinfoil hatters."

"So you're not going to tell her then?"

"And risk her thinking I'm in on the conspiracy? No thanks. I'm hoping you guys can fix this and I won't have to."

I shook my head. "So how come you trust me with this?"

"You just have a way about you. I served with men like you. You're solid."

I gave him a grin as we turned around to go back toward the house and said, "You know you've been the easiest part of my job here. Thank you."

When we got back to the driveway, I stopped at the rental and retrieved the kit from my duffel. Then I followed him up the driveway and in through the garden gate. When he opened the door to let me in, he grinned at me saying, "Welcome to the old fogey's house."

I nodded my thanks, but was taken aback by the subtle shift of atmosphere. Making a mental note of the odd feeling it gave me, I followed Jack to the living room and then began laying out the test kit components. It was just the standard stuff they sent us into the field with: syringe, tweezers, vials, clippers and swabs.

Jack looked like he was ready, so we got the blood test out of the way first. The blood looked perfectly normal as it filled the phials. Then I clipped a bit of fingernail along with a tiny bit of cuticle, and retrieved a hair from his shirt. I went ahead and swabbed his cheek while I was there, to get a sample for easy extraction.

"Thank you so much, Mr. Morris. We'll be in touch with your results."

"Yeah," Jack said, raising his voice just enough that she might hear him from the kitchen, "and tell them if I got some kind of plague or something, I'm definitely suing!"

"Sure thing, Mr. Morris," I said, trying to keep from grinning at his ruse, "Enjoy the rest of your evening."

I went out and got in the car, and was just backing out of the driveway when three black SUVs blocked me in. Putting the car in park, I leaned over to push the kit up under the seat and got out to meet our uninvited guests.

Six guys in SWAT style gear got out and surrounded me. They were equipped with some type of new semi-autos. Hell, they might have been full-on autos. I just knew I didn't want to give them a chance to use them. Two suits were exiting the rear SUV, followed by none other than Hurt himself. The old man greeted me with a sadistic smile.

"Are we feeling any shift in alliances, Mr. Edison?"

"Fuck off."

"Now, this is a nice neighborhood. We wouldn't want to give people the impression you were unrefined—not with your family's history and all."

"I'm sorry," I said, sneering, "I meant fuck off sir. Please."

Light exploded behind my eyes again, but this time I was determined not to go down. This time I wheeled on the goon behind me, bringing up a nice haymaker punch as I turned. The guy lost his grip on reality as well as his grip on the earth. He landed on his ass on the hood of my car, his gun scattering shots in a chaotic arc as he fell.

I spun back around just in time to clip the next guy in the jaw with a left that had just enough momentum to knock him back into the goon immediately on his right. When the guy came back up, I drew his sidearm and popped off two rounds in Hurt's general direction.

"While Hurt was still ducking and his babysitters were still trying to block bullets for him, I hopped in the car and tore out across the lawn, right across Jamie's flower beds. It was the only path, but the little car didn't make the trip unscathed. It scraped hard coming down off the retaining wall, and dragged pieces of fence along behind me for a couple of blocks. There would almost certainly be a leak, but if Hurt's goons followed me, it would be worth it.

When I looked back, they weren't there. My guts did a familiar twisting dance, and I flipped a U-turn. *Fuck. They weren't there for me. They were there for Jack.*

The trucks were gone by the time I got back. I ran into the house to check on Jack and Jamie. Jamie lay across the coffee table in the living room, her head hanging over the edge and tilted at an impossible angle. Blood dripped from a hole on her neck to the carpet. Jack was gone.

There were only a couple of places I could think of to look for him. It was unlikely they would take him back to the tower when they had such a convenient body disposal system back at the Cain's. *Why take Jack?* The engine on the little car was smoking, and the oil light was on. I made for downtown and was about halfway back before it started knocking. I'd have to stop and trade it in at the rental company.

I limped the poor car into the rental place and traded it in for a Jeep. The fee for breaking the car was steep, but at least now I'd be able to get where I needed to go. As I transferred my stuff into the Jeep, I called Therin. I cringed a little when she answered.

"Hey," she said, much more quietly than I expected.

"Therin. Hey. You still interested in working for The Office?"

"You have no idea how much," she said shivering. *Odd, it isn't even that cold...*

"Meet me back at the steel shop."

"That's gonna be a little bit of a problem."

"How come?"

"Mr. Hurt wants me to tell you something."

Suddenly, my head was pounding. The thrumming in my ears reached a level where I almost couldn't hear what she was saying.

"...Meet us once again, and this time, you have to come unarmed or you'll never make it past the first checkpoint, and neither will your little protégé. Remember Mr. Edison, we not only know who you are exactly, exactly—meaning we know your weaknesses—but we also know who you work for – exactly—and what their weaknesses are. One hour." The phone clicked and silence. *So much for the cavalry.*

Why Jack? Surely they weren't just using him to get to me, they could have killed me when they had me before. The disguise had been pretty good, and my phone contacts—was my phone bugged? I pried the back off of the phone. Sure enough, tucked in right next to my SIM card was a micro-transmitter that didn't belong. No one had ever been alone with it except—Claire. Claire bugged my phone. *And the creatures sucked her under and ate her. I led them to Therin, just as surely as I'd led them to Jack, and just as surely as Claire had led them to me.*

I twisted around and unzipped my duffel. Then I took out the notepad and pen and wrote down the number for The Office from my phone. There was a guy coming up the lot to take the Toyota away. I remembered the samples at the last minute and retrieved them, tucking them into the top of my duffel. It wouldn't do to lose those, especially if Jack was lost to me. By the time I got there he may well be. Grinding my molars, I put the Jeep in gear and headed for the nearest truck stop.

TWELVE

When I walked in the door at the truck stop, the smell of bacon and eggs hit me like a gut-punch. I instinctively inhaled every last delicious scent. Coffee. Sausage. Something sweet. Syrup? French toast? *When was the last time I ate?* Though I had no time to eat, I needed to—and I needed a cover for being here. I nabbed one of the free magazines by the door and headed for a booth in a fairly crowded section.

I ordered the special and coffee and opened the magazine so I could pretend to read. Hey, it's a cliché for a reason. I listened to the conversations all around me. One guy was on the phone with his wife, saying he'd be home soon, and one of the truckers was talking to another trucker about the best way to haul on ice and snow, since he was getting ready to go to Canada.

After I listened for a good ten minutes, breakfast arrived and I scarfed down as much of it as I could before the driver going to Canada got up to pay his check.

I felt for the poor sap if Hurt actually went after him, and I hoped I hadn't just got another innocent person killed. I picked up my own check and followed the man to the cashier. I waited patiently, exchanged pleasantries with the clerk and watched to see which truck the guy got into.

Making for the back of the row of trucks, I did my best to look like I was just passing by them all at once on my way to somewhere else. I stopped briefly at the back of the man's truck and slipped the phone onto the flat hollow space between the back bumper and the trailer chassis. I had no way to attach it there, but hoped it would at least travel far enough to keep Hurt and his goons off me until I got to the Cain's.

I had five minutes to spare when I pulled the jeep into the parking lot. I felt naked walking in without my sidearm, but I had resources they couldn't check at the door. No way was that sonofabitch taking another person out on my watch.

The woman behind the bar had a goon with her this time. They frisked me and we did the metal detector mambo before they let me pass.

"What, no cavity search?"

The guy with the metal detector wand smiled a small evil smile, and the woman said, "Don't tempt us, sugar. He's waiting."

There was nothing in the hallway I could use as a weapon, not even a picture for broken glass, or a table I could break up for beatin' sticks. I opened the door to the office to find that Jack and Therin were still alive, but each had blood pooling under their seat.

They were the only ones in the room that I could see, and all of the furniture besides the two chairs they were taped to had been removed. They sat perched on the same damn trap door I'd fallen down only hours ago.

When I stepped across the threshold, a solid steel sheet slammed down behind me. Rolling my eyes, I went to free Therin first. I bent to undo the tape that held her right arm to the chair. *There must be some irritant in the air, my damn eyes keep watering.* Therin was struggling, doing her best to call out from behind the tape on her mouth.

"I am so sorry Therin, really I am."

That arm free, I began working on her legs. She'd been crying. Right now however, she was busy tapping on my shoulder with her free hand. Finally she used her free hand to rip the tape from her mouth.

"It's—"

"Yeah. I know."

The tape around her ankles finally gave way. "You finish this up, I'm going to start on Jack."

"So good to see you again Mr. Edison," Hurt's voice buzzed in my ears. "You have a very important decision to make."

"I've already made it."

"I'd like to help you reconsider before things become—irreversible. You are on the wrong side of things."

"Says the serial killer..."

I kept at the tape on Jack's arm, and after giving him a pointed look and whispering to him, "I'm sorry," I stood and turned to face the voice behind me.

"Soldier," Hurt said, his voice from the television as steady as if he were giving a classroom lecture or a boardroom presentation. It was the kind of cool conviction often heard from extremist clergy right before something got blown up. "This is a war, and we could use a man of your obvious talents."

"Which talents would those be—exactly, Mr. Hurt? You don't mind if I call you 'Reg' do ya?"

"Well actually..."

"Just what kind of war are you running here anyway *Reg*? Most wars have guns, tanks, surface-to-air missiles and something else—what was it—oh yeah—a *purpose*. What the hell is the *purpose* of all this? What do you really *want*?"

"Why, the future of the human race, and the earth itself! The world is crying for change and for heroes, and I know that's what is in your heart or you wouldn't be here."

"You know jack shit about me, or being a hero—not that I am one. You are a murdering little psychopath without a shred of decency. I have no time for your shit."

"You have no idea what's coming."

"So tell the jury. Or Satan, because when I find you, and I will find you, you're not going to have to worry about sitting in a cell with Bubba."

The face on the screen grimaced and his right shoulder seemed to twitch. I jumped, but didn't have enough oomph to make the edge of the trapdoor. All three of us fell. Therin yelped, but Jack didn't make a sound. I landed badly, wrenching one knee, but the others likely had it worse.

"Therin," I called into the darkness, "Jack?"

I heard Therin moan, but still nothing from Jack. He was probably much weaker than Therin right now, due to his age and condition. *But what is his condition?* I crawled along the damp stone, following Therin's moaning to where she lay, my eyes slowly adjusting to the dark. When I got to her, I reached out a hand to find her face. What I found instead was a breast. Brushing aside the embarrassment, I continued upward to find her face. I could just make her out now in the gloom, and I cast my eyes around the tunnel for Jack.

"Thank you for coming to get me, she said, shaking still.

"Don't thank anybody yet," I told her. "You haven't seen the things that live down here."

"Jack?" I called it out softly, and heard a muffled moan in return. Following the voice I could just make him out by the water's edge. I scrambled over and pulled him and his chair away from the already churning water. That done, I pulled the tape off his mouth.

"Max. Thank you, son."

"We're not out of the shit yet, sir. Can you walk?"

"I'm not sure. I've bled a lot."

"Okay, let's deal with that first."

"You said we hadn't seen what's down here..."

"Some kind of eel sucker-fish things and fanged flying fish, and something bigger. In the water— but they can jump. I've never seen anything like 'em."

"You need to get the lady out of here."

"Sure, we'll go in a minute. Let's get you guys' bleeding stopped so we don't get the fish jumping."

"There's no time for that."

"Sir..."

"You've been in close combat?"

I nodded and then realized he couldn't see it. "Yes."

"Does the enemy sit and wait for you to patch each other up?"

"No but..."

"Same principle. These guys aren't going to sit around and wait for you to come back at them with healed wounds. Take it from me, just get as far as possible away from these jackdaws, and then deal with her injuries.

Come back at 'em hard with as much backup as possible. Tell Jamie I love her, and what really happened. Tell her I went down fighting for someone else's freedom. Now help me up."

"Sir..."

"And quit calling me sir. Grab that chair arm and hand it here. You are going to need someone to run interference if you want to get out alive."

"Yes sir," I said. Those damned irritants were stinging my eyes again.

I grabbed the chair arm and helped Jack to his feet, then went back to check on (*Gods, don't die...*) Therin. She was watching, entranced, as the water roiled and the pale glistening bodies of the creatures writhed just beneath the surface, whipped into a frenzy by the scent of blood in the water.

Maybe that was the idea behind cutting the arteries—aside from a relatively swift and painless death. Those things would make quick work of their dirty laundry.

At least she hadn't been dumped directly into the water. Maybe they didn't have real good aim from TV land. I took off my long-sleeve shirt and tied it securely around Therin's upper thigh. She didn't move to stop me and she didn't even make a snide remark about me supposedly copping a feel. She just stared at the water.

"Hey," I said, touching her cheek and gently turning her to face me. "How about you and me get out of here and go somewhere a little nicer?"

"Sure," she said, seeming to look through me, "that sounds great."

I twined an arm around her midsection and scooped her up. I could carry her as far as the crossing point I'd used earlier, but I had no clue how I was supposed to get her across. It wasn't a long jump, but she'd need to build up energy if she was going to make it on her own. In her weakened state, it might just be too far. There was no way I could jump with her in my arms.

When I got to the manhole ladder I'd climbed up before, it was freshly welded shut. They knew where I'd got out before, and made sure I couldn't do that again. Knowing they were probably watching, I glanced down the tunnel at the corners of the ceiling. Sure enough. Cameras everywhere.

There was no move I could make that they wouldn't be watching. Since destroying the cameras would probably only bring Hurt and the goons back, I left them alone for the time being and carried Therin back to where we'd left Jack.

Jack was dead. The creatures in the water hadn't come out to get him. Yet.

THIRTEEN

"Jack was a good guy and he's dead because of me," I said, turning to Therin. "You are hurt, and who knows how many others— I'm sorry..."

"Shut up. You didn't do this. Besides we don't have time for you to throw a pity party, I'm pretty sure I ain't far behind if we don't move."

"Can you walk?"

"Yeah."

"Can you fight?"

"I think so."

I set her on her feet and said, "We have to try this way, but it's liable to get hairy. You good?"

"I've got some skills. I've seen better days though, so no promises, 'kay?"

"Fair enough." I handed her the 2x4 so she could use it to lean on or swing, whatever she needed. She was bleeding slower now, but still bleeding. She'd need real help soon, or she'd be just as dead as Claire and Jack—and that was if the monsters didn't get her.

We made our way back down the tunnel toward the pool. I didn't want to know what was lurking in the deep water there, but there had to be another exit, and it had to be this way. I only hoped we could find it before we became dinner. The pool had grown calm in our absence.

I motioned for Therin to stay still and quiet, while I took soft, careful steps along the narrowing ledge beside the water.

There was a wall that ended our walkway, but it only cut about three feet into the pool, and then jogged back about four or five feet. The tunnel went on behind the chain link, but there was also a solid area that looked like a landing and a dark area beyond that could be stairs. There was something leaning against the wall in the landing, but it was too far to tell what it was in the gloom. The Chain link went from one side to the other here, just like the other end, but as the now lightly roiling water moved, it exposed the raw end of the chain link just at the top of the water. It didn't go all the way down like the other side.

"Okay," I said, feeling that old familiar gut-sink and adrenaline kick, "Next question. Can you swim?"

"Yeah some," she said. Then she realized what that meant and her eyes got wide. "In there? Oh *hell* no."

"It's the only way out."

"It's suicide."

"Maybe." I looked around the tunnel one last time. There was only one other thing here that might help us.

"Maybe not," I said, "But you're not gonna like it. Hell, I don't like it."

"Tell me."

"We're going to feed them before we get in."

"What the hell?" She followed my eyes as I cast a nod and a glance in the direction of Jack's body. "No!"

"He's our only out."

"It's inhuman."

She was shivering harder, and looking a lot like a child. I couldn't help it. She made me feel like a heel. I had to find a way for her to accept what had to be done, and it had to be fast.

"It's what he would want," I said, laying my hands lightly on her trembling shoulders, "He was willing to offer his life for our escape. He wouldn't want you stuck down here. Now come on."

"But they didn't get him yet, maybe they don't want him," she said.

"I think he was out of their reach. Either that or they hunt by vibration. I saw them eat Claire's body before, so I know they eat carrion. Therin, we have to try. We can't just stay here— you need help." For an instant I wondered if Claire had felt it when that thing dragged her under.

Therin nodded and I dropped my hands from her shoulders. Handing her the chair-rung stake, I turned to go and scoot Jack over to the water. Therin's voice stopped me.

"I can swim, but wouldn't it be better to climb?"

"Do what?"

"Climb. That chain link comes all the way to the end of the walkway. It's bolted to the concrete, so it should hold us. If we climb out to the middle on it, then just duck under we might actually make it."

"It sure would save us some time," I said, feeling a the beginnings of a smile for the first time in a while. "You know, you're pretty handy to have around."

"So I'm told," she said, flashing me a quick grin in return. "It still might not be enough though."

"No, but it's our best shot. Let me know when you're ready."

"Let's just do it."

"I'll go get Jack."

The lamprey creatures were jumping by the time I got to Jack's body. They seemed to have a maximum jump of about a foot. Still too far for comfort. Jack was heavier than I would have thought, but I managed to get him close enough to the edge that I could roll him off without too much trouble. If I could get the majority of the feeding frenzy at this end, we might stand a chance.

I looked to Therin. She nodded and I tipped him up and pushed his shoulders over the edge just far enough that he would finish sliding in on his own. That done, I ran as quietly as possible back to where she was already scaling the chain link. A glance over my shoulder told me that the creatures had already stared devouring Jack. With a shudder, I climbed onto the fencing with Therin.

"Climb on my back," I said. "It'll be faster if I can swing us both under at the same time."

She complied without argument, and as she clung to me shivering, I climbed down the fence to crouch at the water's surface. I looked at the water, but it was so full of blood that I couldn't tell if there were creatures beneath us or not.

"Here we go," I told her, and inhaled as deeply as possible with her arms around my neck. I felt her inhale too, and let my legs down into the water, I grabbed hold of the bottom of the fencing and kicked as hard as I could, pulling and kicking with everything I had to get us across. As I kicked, my foot grazed something and I lunged for the surface. I climbed, heaving for air, and pulling for both of us, until we hung just above the water. So far so good. The red water churned below us though, and I kept us moving toward the landing, creeping sideways like a crab. Once there, Therin clambered from my back and onto the fence. Then she jumped over onto the landing, nearly tipping back over into the water. Involuntarily I reached a hand in her direction, but she was too far away. Once she righted herself, I made to follow her.

That was when the tentacle curled around my right ankle. That was when I realized that there were claws on the tentacles of the thing beneath me, as they bit into my flesh. Startled by its relative stealth and strength, I yelped. My own strength was flagging and I began to think I was the one who was done for. The bloody water churned more and more violently as my own blood joined with it.

The wire bit into my hands, and the tentacle was soon joined by another on my other leg, this one at knee height. I pulled against it, working toward the landing. Another tentacle joined the first one on my right foot and yanked it off the fence.

"Gah!"

"Max!" It was Therin's voice from behind me.

I couldn't spare the focus of turning to look at her. I was losing ground. The thing was pulling me down. Worse, it was putting fresh blood in the water. My blood. The lampreys started to jump. A new tentacle wrapped around my neck, and I slid several links down the fence before I got a grip again. Something hit me in my lower back, and there was a sharp pain there. My vision blurred. A new tentacle slithered around my left thigh and up around my torso.

I was ready. At least Therin might get out. I tried to get one last breath, but only got burning for my effort. It was time to let go.

Just then there were two sounds that I couldn't reconcile in my mind with anything I knew. They weren't gunshots. Was it a bow? No, too mechanical. Nail gun? No. Too big.

As I clung to the fence, suffocating, bleeding, and trying to make out the sounds I was hearing, a third and fourth sound rang out. It was metallic, mechanical and large. The tentacles all loosened at once. Air blossomed in my lungs. Foul as it was, it was the best thing ever.

"Max! Come on!"

As my brain started putting things together again, I realized that it was Therin's voice. I was free of the tentacles, and though I was still bleeding and there was still a weight and pressure in my back, I could move again. I reached the landing in less than a minute, and dragged my injured ass onto it. I immediately hit my knees. I was weak.

Therin made me lay on my stomach. How was she so much stronger than me? There were squelching sounds from behind (above?) me, and the pain left my back. The dank walls spun and drifted away. I couldn't have been out more than a minute, because when things swam back into focus, Therin was there, and she had my head in her lap.

She sat with her back against the farthest wall, and she was breathing like she, too, was asleep. One of the lamprey creatures lay just off to the right, its head sloppily severed from its body. A harpoon gun and a knife lay close to her and I finally realized what that sound had been. The thing in the shadows, the metallic sound, had been her firing the harpoon gun at the monster that was trying to eat me. She'd saved my life.

I didn't want to wake her, so I sat up slowly. The claws on that thing had left deep gouges in my skin and each one was its own hell. The lamprey bite was still pretty well numb, so at least it didn't hurt. I couldn't see it though, so I didn't know how much it might still be bleeding. I looked around, turning my head gingerly on my sore neck. There were stairs alright. One set leading up and one set leading down.

The upstairs probably led back to the night club, and right back into Hurt's clutches. Once we were on the surface, I could at least fight to keep us there as long as we were together. She was sleeping deeply, and I felt like a heel, but I reached over and shook her gently. Her eyes sprung open so wide and so fast it made me flinch. Then I froze.

That was a look that guys got in the field. The look that said they just might deal some damage to whatever moves the wrong way. When her eyes relaxed into recognition, I let my arm come back to my side.

"I have to go look at the downstairs. You want to rest here while I check it out?"

"I think I'll stay with you if it's all the same."

"It's probably dangerous, and you're in no shape..."

She looked me up and down. "And you are? Fucking idiot."

I chuckled in spite of the pain. Then I grunted as I shoved myself up off the floor, and stuck out a hand for her to grab. She pulled up, favoring the injured leg a lot. Once she got to her feet, though, she let go of my hand and took her own weight.

She struggled a little going down the stairs, but at the bottom, she and I both just stood in a sort of disbelief for a moment before continuing on into the well-furnished room. It was sumptuous. The would-be windows were draped in dark red velvet, and there was a decorative soapstone mantle set against the far wall. This surrounded a large flat screen that likely had cable and maybe internet when it wasn't standing in for a real fireplace.

At the front of the chamber stood a baby grand piano. In the back corner was a bar, and in the opposite corner, a desk and a file cabinet. The walls were lined with books. The desk was where I headed first. The top of the desk was littered with papers and clippings of articles that detailed occurrences of high strangeness. The same types of things we investigated at The Office.

Laid out across the computer's keyboard was a piece of very old-looking parchment with foreign writing, and below that a large sheet of vellum to which were glued five smaller sheets of papyrus containing hieroglyphs. A great blue ankh adorned the top center of the vellum, connected to each of the papyri by thick black lines. Therin plopped into the cushioned chair behind me, and it drew me out of my fascination with the strange papers.

When she did, I cast a glance around the room and decided all of it had to go with us. There were leather scrolls and paper ones, wax tubes with writing on them, and even clay tablets with what was probably cuneiform writing on them. Statues of strange deities and monsters from various mythologies graced the shelves in between the books.

Above the shelves were tools and weapons of the sort used in ancient times to inflict horrors upon their victims.

I looked around for something to put all this stuff in. No bag jumped out at me, so I grabbed one of the larger leather rolls and opened it up. Without looking to see what was written there, I began laying the parchments, vellums and other assorted scrolls inside it. That was when my hands found it. It was an enormous three-ring binder laid open under the stacks. Across the pages lay a crescent-bladed knife, the wicked point covered in drying blood. Maybe Therin's blood. I paused to read the words written there.

"...and the chalice of flesh shall run over, and the Earth shall become the chalice, and all flesh and blood shall pour into her and all flesh will mingle therein. The human scourge shall cease to rule the lands, and all shall be made one. Magic will be reborn unto the world."

So the dude was an eco-terrorist? It fit. Sort of. There had to be more to it, but I didn't have time to figure it out. I stuck the binder and the knife in the leather and bound it up with the leather lacings. Then I offered Therin my hand and she stood. Whatever Hurt was planning, it would have to wait until after the emergency room.

FOURTEEN

By the time I had everything ready to head up the stairs, Therin had passed out in the chair behind me. I shook her gently, but she didn't stir. Cussing under my breath, I rigged a carrying strap on the bundle from the harpoon and slung it over my shoulder. Then I lifted her as carefully as possible onto my back and made for the stairs.

By the time I hit the landing, my muscles were on fire. By the time I made the door at the top of the stairs, they were screaming. We came out behind the bar. Pale morning light gleamed sleepily through the cracks in the drawn blinds. We'd been down there all night, but at least there was no one in the bar to challenge our escape. When we got to the parking lot, the Jeep was gone. Hurt probably had it towed, thinking we were dead.

Fearing I would drop her or fall with her, I finally eased Therin onto the pavement. I felt for a pulse. It was there, but it was weak. I had to sit for a second, but then I picked her back up and headed out to the street. There weren't many cars out this time of the morning, and as I carried her, her head lolling over my arm, two cars passed us by. Women. Women never stopped. Good for them. Then a man passed us. Never even slowed. That pissed me off.

I got madder with every step after that, and by the time I heard the next engine rumbling up behind us, I was madder than hell. The big black pickup rumbled to a stop beside us, and all that anger drained off like water, only to be replaced by a sudden desperation, and a gratitude that choked me up some.

The big Native-American man in the driver's seat leaned over and pushed open the passenger door, then got out and ran around to help me get her up in the seat.

"Thank you."

He nodded and ran back around to hop in. I climbed up into the cab and rested her head on my shoulder so I could hold her upright and he could drive.

"What happened to her?" He asked the question while looking but pretending not to look. He was pretending to focus on putting the truck in gear.

"Long story," I said, shivering now in the cool morning air. "Can we just get her to a hospital?"

"Sure."

We arrived pretty quick, having been just a few miles away; and when he pulled up, I jumped out to go grab a wheelchair. When I came back, the guy was already getting Therin out of the truck. He eased her into the chair, and then walked ahead of us to open the doors as I wheeled her in.

"Hey!" I hollered when we got into the check-in area, "Can we get someone out here? I think she's dying!"

A middle-aged hulking man in scrubs came out of the double triage doors like he'd been shot out of a cannon. The look on his face was somewhere between wanting to punch my lights out and getting to the bottom of all this racket. Once his eyes landed on Therin, all questions were laid aside. He nodded and went to hold the doors open.

I pushed the chair to the doors, but never made it past the threshold. The big guy swooped in and took over pushing the chair as another person's arm looped around my shoulders and led me in another direction. I pulled back. I wasn't ready to be examined just yet.

"Sir, I need to take a look at you too."

"Sure, just let me thank the guy that brought us in."

I looked around for the big guy, but he wasn't there. I strode to the outer doors, and peeked out to find him outside, pacing. I went out, the nurse shouting at my back not to leave. The guy didn't even look up. He grunted an acknowledgement of my existence, leaving the opening of conversation to me.

"Thanks again, man. Hey, I didn't catch your name."

"I didn't give it." At this, he did look up, and gave me a quick once-over as he did. He must have decided I was alright, because he gave me a nod and stuck out one massive hand. "Kane Quinn. Bounty hunter."

I felt an eyebrow pop up. I shook his hand and said, "Wow, that sounds like tons of fun."

"Has its moments. And you are..."

"Federal agent Maxwell Edison."

"Seriously? Maxwell Edison?"

"Yeah, why?"

"Majoring in medicine?"

"No..."

"You mean you've never heard that song?"

"What song?"

"Maxwell's silver hammer. It's The Beatles, man."

"I don't really do a lot of music."

"That's sacrilege." He spit something on the sidewalk, and looked at his feet, shaking his head.

"Hey look, this place is going to be crawling with cops here in a minute. I've got to call somebody from my office to come and pick this stuff up." I patted the leather bundle at my side. "Do you think you could stick around here until they show? If they haul me in, I'd really rather not have to explain, and I need this to get back to my office. It's evidence."

"Sure man, just show me that badge. Sorry, I've been burned."

"No problem." I fished my wallet out and showed him my ID card. "We don't really get the shiny metal ones. We don't get the big bucks."

"Looks legit, I guess," Quinn said, but then he put one finger dead center in my chest and said in a clearly threatening manner, "But—you screw me over and I won't hesitate to kick the living shit out of you before I turn you in."

"Understood," I said, handing the bag over. Quinn cocked an eyebrow at me, but said nothing. He got back in the truck and I went back into the ER to face the music.

The nurse who had taken my arm looked relieved, but I walked right past her and to the admissions counter which I reached over to grab the phone off of the desk. The lady behind the admissions desk started to say something, but I gave her a look of warning and she backed off.

I dialed nine and then punched in the number for The Office.

"Toni, may I help you?"

"Hey Toni. It's me."

"Max?"

"Yeah, look, I'm up shit creek here. I'm going to need some backup."

"Where are you?"

"At a hospital in Tulsa. I'll either be in jail or back at the hotel by the time you send someone."

"We're all coming."

"Say what?"

"I'll explain when I see you, but we're moving ops to Oklahoma. I'll be landing in a few minutes with Arlan, Dr. Pape and Mr. Chamberlain. We've got some of the security team with us now."

"These guys are big-time, but I have a feeling that Hurt answers to this Shadow Council. There's a guy in the parking lot with the evidence. Do you have anyone left close by who can come get it?"

"Just one. I'll get him on the way."

"Good." I couldn't help the big sigh that followed. This shit was starting to catch up with me. Blue and red lights bounced around the walls. "I've got to go. Looks like the police are here."

"Just behave," she said, "and show them your ID. We'll put in a call to vouch for you, but it still might take a little bit."

"I'm at the Super Inn just outside Sapulpa for now. Room 308."

"See you soon."

"See ya."

I walked around the corner just as an officer was striding up the hall in search of me. I flipped open my wallet and handed it to him so he could inspect my ID. The room was starting to spin a little bit by the time he handed it back.

"Maxwell Edison," I said, the lightheadedness draining the authority from my voice. "I'm with the government."

"I'm going to need you to come with me, sir."

"Of course."

We were about halfway back to the lobby when the pain gripped my chest again and I couldn't breathe. The officer ahead of me, along with the entire hospital, swung sickeningly sideways and then disappeared into blackness.

When I came to, I felt like I was coming off a really vicious tequila drunk. One during which I got hit in the chest with a sledgehammer. I was no longer anywhere near the lobby, but still in the hospital. Looked like maybe I was in ICU. The walls were all glass and there were machines hooked to me everywhere. There was a uniformed man standing outside the door, and a tall man in plain clothes. His body language painted him as cop, though.

I wondered if he knew it was obvious. Machines started beeping in protest as I attempted to sit up and found myself restrained. A nurse scurried in the door, pausing briefly to exchange with the men at the door. The detective turned to study me through the glass.

The nurse babbled about lying still and they were expecting test results and it would be just a few minutes and the doctor would be in, but I barely heard her. I watched the intent face of the detective. Something about him pissed me off. Something in the way he held his jaw. Some cruelty behind his eyes made me want to cut through the restraints with my teeth if necessary and put those eyes out. Permanently.

The restraints held good, and eventually the babbling nurse went back out, and on the way, she pulled the curtains around my cube, effectively blocking his view.

I heard her stop in the doorway again and hiss angrily at the men about not bothering her patients and they could wait out in recovery. I gave in to the power of gravity and relaxed a little. The bed was pretty comfy, and the last few days had caught up to me. I must have dozed then, because I came back around again when the door opened and a plump, middle-aged doctor with a balding pate and a pocket protector walked in and pulled the chart off the foot of the bed.

"Mr Edison," he said, in the usual detached courteous voice doctors seem to share, "you have a lot of 'splaining to do."

I grunted. It seemed appropriate.

"You have some interesting stuff going on," he continued, "and until I get some info, I am at a loss to explain it."

He hooked a foot around one of those little roll-y stools that occupied a crowded corner of the cube, positioned it near the head of the bed and plopped on it. He studied me for a minute, smiling his faint, detached smile, so I grunted again to acknowledge him. He went on...

"Given the description of the pain that you gave in your delirious state, we did a chest x-ray after we got you sedated, and there is a sliver of bone lodged in your chest that doesn't seem to come from anywhere in your body."

"The fuck?"

"That's what we said. Can you shed any light on that for me?"

"Well, yeah, maybe. But they said there was only one."

The doctor cocked an eyebrow, his detachment giving way to genuine interest.

"I was in Afghanistan. The bone sliver is from my buddy. We got blown up together, only he didn't make it. They took out one sliver. I guess they missed a piece."

"I guess so. We missed it on our initial scans. Thing is, Mr. Edison, I'm not sure we can take it out without killing you."

"Excuse me?"

"It's very, very close. I daresay I'd put it within one-one-hundredths of an inch. And it's surrounded by scar tissue. In your current state it would be risky at best. Right now, we think the majority of your pain was caused by exertion and exacerbation of the original injury leading to general inflammation around the heart and scar tissue. In short, you just need to take it easy for a while."

"Yeah," I said, the word gushing out with an exasperated sigh. "That's gonna happen. I can't do this. I can't be here. There are people depending on me."

"And how much good will you do them from a casket? I'm admitting you. At least overnight for observation. We'll see where you are in the morning." He must have seen my defiance all over my face, because he grinned then and said, "and the restraints are staying on until we're sure you won't take off."

"What about the girl I came in with?"

"She's stable. She flat lined a couple of times, but we're confident she'll pull through. We're giving her blood and pushing fluids. She owes you her life, Mr. Edison."

"She doesn't owe me anything. Can somebody keep an eye on her?"

"I'll let you ask the police officers that. There's a detective who's been waiting since last night for a statement. Can I tell him to come in or to come back later?"

"Tell him to come in. Though if it's that asshole from last night, he'll be glad you got me tied down."

"Okay. Just try not to get too worked up or we'll wind up keeping you longer."

"Right."

The doctor went out, and within seconds, the door opened again. The weasel-faced man from earlier slid into my room and was standing beside me before I could say hello.

"You the guy that brought in the dead chick?"

"Is she dead? Did she die? Fuck!" I strained against the restraints again, but to no avail.

"Well, she flat-lined a couple times. They say she's stable now, though." He grinned smugly around the toothpick he held between his teeth.

"Damn dude."

"You want to tell me what happened to her?"

"Reginald Hurt and his band of trained baboons happened to her."

"You mean the billionaire philanthropist Reginald Hurt?" He looked like I told him the sky was chartreuse with purple polka-dots.

"Only if his middle name is Arcturis and he's the third one."

His jaw worked, and I could see he was struggling not to call me out directly. "You know he's like seventy-five right? What's he gonna do?"

"Make a small incision. He's got hired help for the rest."

"You got any evidence?"

"I've got my testimony and hers, if she can pull through. That's all you get. By the way, how does someone like good old Reg. get away with so many obviously criminal acts in one city for so long, *detective*? He backed up and put his fists on the sides of his hips, widening his stance.

"Now look. I'm the one asking—"

"No. Afraid not, pal. I've got jurisdiction. This is a federal investigation and you're cramping my style. So shove off."

"Sure," he said, grinding his teeth into the toothpick as his whole head turned red, "I'll just need a copy of that ID, a written statement, and for you to pass clearance." Right then his cell phone rang and he took a deep breath as he pulled it out of its little holster and swiped the screen. There were a couple of yes's, a no, and a final "fine" before he tapped the screen and looked at me directly. The rage was as plain at the deepening red of his face. He said very quietly, "What was your name?"

"*Agent* Maxwell Edison. I trust that was a call from my office?" Some of the red drained out of his face. He nodded, but still looked suspicious. It could have just been the way his face was made though.

"You'll have the department's full cooperation. I trust you'll keep us advised of any new developments?"

"Oh, sure," I said, not completely sarcastically, "And could you put a couple of guys on Therin's room? I have a feeling Hurt's not done with her yet."

"We already have. Anything else?"

"No. I'm sorry if this has disrupted your carefully constructed worldview, but there are things going on that you can't understand, and it's bigger than your precious city. I'm going after Hurt. If I can't bring him in alive, I'm bringing him in dead. Is that a problem?

"Not as long as you're legit." He slid the phone back into its little holster and turned toward the door, then he turned back and fixed me with a level stare. "If you're not though, I'll bury you, and I'll do it with this town's blessing."

"Fair enough. Anything else you need? I've got to get out of this and go find Therin."

"Just don't go too far."

"You kidding? I am *so* out of here."

FIFTEEN

The woman at the nurse's desk tried to give me the "We can't give out personal information" speech when I was allowed to wheel myself out to go find Therin the next morning. They still wouldn't let me walk, though I felt perfectly capable. This was one time I was able to pull rank on my own. Even from a wheelchair when the words "federal" and "investigation" come out, people tend to pay attention to the words that follow.

I wasn't crazy about pulling rank, but there was shit that needed to get done. It was one thing to aim a gun at a killer, but somehow flashing the badge to get my way seemed like taking advantage. Mama Vierna would not approve, and when Mama Vierna did not approve, the waters were treacherous indeed.

The desk nurse wound up pushing the chair to Therin's room. "She's breathing on her own again," she said, "though it was touch and go for a while last night."

"Can I call and check on her later?"

"Of course. I'll leave a note for my relief."

"Thank you," I said as she swung the door open, "Um, what was your name again?"

"Leslie, sir," she said, pushing her long black braid back over her shoulder, "Leslie Birch" She was almost a negative image of Claire. Dark-skinned and black haired, where Claire had been pale and blond.

"Thank you Leslie. Also, I'm afraid I'll be checking out today, even if it's against doctors' recommendation. There are some very serious matters I have to attend to."

"Does it have something to do with that lizard-man on the television?"

"Lizard-man?"

"They said he had green scales and funky spikes growing out his back." And all at once lovely Leslie turned into the host of "That's Unbelievable!" as she told the story as she knew it. "They said he was running all over downtown, trying to get away from everybody. Made a bad crossing on 3rd and Boston and caused a big wreck. One guy in a truck jumped the sidewalk and hit a building, and then—"

"Wow, actually that's news to me, but it might be connected. Can you arrange for my release?"

"Sure. You go get 'em. You're just like that guy in 'Weird Files,' huh?"

"Yeah..."

She parked me beside Therin's bed and scuttled back out the door. My ears were burning. As I breathed a sigh of relief and felt the fire in my earlobes begin to subside, I looked over at Therin. She seemed to be comfortable, but she was so pale, so fragile-looking. So tiny.

Then I remembered what that tiny woman could do. As much as I wanted to protect her, I knew that The Office might still see her as a threat. *No way am I saying anything about her abilities yet. She's my asset and right now, that takes precedence over study and the risk of her running amok.* I couldn't look at her and think of what they might do to her. I wheeled myself back to my room, gathered up my clothes and got dressed in the bathroom after a nice hot shower.

When I exited the hospital, Quinn's truck was gone. Toni's agent would have long since come and gone with the package I'd entrusted to Quinn. There was a long silver Lincoln in the lot that I recognized immediately as Dr. Pape's. *How in the hell did they get here so fast? How in the hell did they get the car here that fast?*

Toni got out of the passenger side and motioned me over. I hesitated, their sudden appearance was a little too much to swallow without coffee or bourbon. Dr. Pape poked her head out the passenger rear window with a bright, reassuring smile.

"You've had a rough couple of days, Max," she said. "What have you been stirring up here?"

"A lot of shit," I said, walking on over, but not standing too close to the car. "How did you get here so fast? Toni said something about relocating?"

"Yes, as this is the densest area of anomalous activity, and our construction site in Maryland was destroyed, we've decided to get a little closer to the action, so to speak."

"Well, you're in the middle of it now. People are dropping like flies around here. Did you catch up with the evidence?"

"No, we haven't talked to anyone yet, we came straight here." She looked around the parking lot and nodded to a man that was approaching us. "Here he comes now."

It was none other than my old buddy Kai Makana from the Corps. Though he looked vaguely like any young man of Asian descent, Kai was actually Hawaiian. Last time I saw him he'd had a girl waiting on the big island with a name I couldn't pronounce. I had some fond face-chat memories of her trying to teach me. She was amazing. I could see why he didn't re-enlist after Fallujah. Kai had been the only one besides me to survive the IED and he looked none the worse. Where I had deep scars, some of which showed around my collar and upper arms, he just had a few lighter spots on perfectly smooth skin. I was glad he got out. Especially now, seeing the grin spreading across his face.

Kai handed off the makeshift bag to Toni and beamed at me.

"Makana," I said, grinning back.

"Edison. Chased any new skirts?"

"Nah," I said. "It was either skirts or liquor, and you know I gotta have my booze."

"More's the pity, man. Looks like you could use a drink now though."

"Hell yeah. Good to see you man, great to have you on the team. I'm just gonna go check on the girl one more time..."

"No Max," Dr. Pape said. "You have to debrief us and we need to get you a new phone. And a hat."

"Claire bugged my phone," I said, searching her face for clues.

"We wondered if she could be our leak. That's why we put her with you."

"What?"

"We knew if she was the mole, you'd expose her and she would cease to be a problem."

"You knew she was going to get killed." Ice and fire ran down my back and raced each other back up my neck.

"The price of treason."

"I'm sorry, but who the *hell* made us judges?"

"Our mandate allows the use of deadly force to protect the human race. If we are compromised and destroyed from the inside, that agenda cannot be accomplished. Therefore it is our implied power and duty to use whatever means necessary to defend The Office of Human Protection and all of its agents and personnel."

"Nice rhetoric."

"Indeed. Now will you please get in the car?"

I nodded goodbye to Kai and got in. Kai watched me unblinking until I was safely in the car, then returned my nod. As bad as shit was getting for agents, I had to wonder if I'd ever see him alive again. I wondered if he was thinking the same thing.

***

Instead of going back to the Super Inn, Dr. Pape thought we'd be better off in a larger establishment, so we wound up at the Mariott. The Mariott wasn't particularly packed, but then it was still Wednesday. The posters in the entryway told me that the sci-fi convention this weekend would probably fill it up pretty quick. The proximity of the hotel made it a convenient staging area, without being so close as to be obvious.

Light misty rain had begun to fall by the time we got out. Arlan, in the lead, opened the right door for Dr. Pape and Toni. For an old guy, he sure got around quick. He had to be in his eighties, but he moved faster than I did—at least today he did.

We converged on the front desk and Dr. Pape made our room arrangements. The ladies would bunk in a room together, as would Arlan and I. For the first time, I realized that Chamberlain wasn't among us. I wondered where the little weasel was. Maybe he didn't make it. A pang of guilt washed over me. Mama Vierna would have smacked me for thinking ill of the possibly deceased. Once everything was agreed upon, Dr. Pape handed us all our room keys.

"We have exclusive use of the meeting room for the next two days. We will meet there in the mornings, bring your breakfast with you. Follow me and I'll show you where it is." She led us around the left side of the lobby and down a narrow, somewhat dimmer hall to a glass fronted door, which she swung open and led us all into. Once we'd all filed in, she turned to address us all again.

"You all know why we're here. We don't have a ton of funding as usual, but the publicity from the explosion and the recent spate of activity have landed us a fair land grant and a little bit of pull with the local officials. We're going to start rebuilding within the week, if we can find an appropriate location. Until then, we're kind of working out of out suitcases with our wits as our primary weapons. We don't even have our basic equipment or sensors. All of that was on the new site when it blew."

"So what we're flying blind? Hell, not even blind but buck naked?"

"Not really naked," she said, eyeing me coolly. "We still have the numbers and some of the arsenal, not to mention Arlan's library, which is still in shipment from Birmingham. We still have communication with the old office and our personal laptops. It's going to be kind of old school with a twist. Max, tell us about this, if you could." She gestured to Toni, who had carried the evidence bundle in without me even noticing. Toni placed the bundle on the table in front of me. I untied the leather straps and the whole mess fell open with a flap. I flipped through the contents looking most specifically for the wickedly curved ritual knife. It wasn't there.

As tight as I'd rolled it, the knife should have been there. I could still see the indentations in the papers of the sharp tip and the rings for the handle and the dimple where the pommel had been. It had been taken. I heaved a sigh and felt my shoulders drop.

"Fuck me."

"What is it?" Toni asked.

"The knife is gone."

Dr. Pape reached around me and pulled out the file folder with the information of The Office. Arlan reached into the pile as well, and pulled out the parchment with the chalice of blood writing on it. Each of them were immediately absorbed with the items they'd selected. Toni just stared at me.

"There was this small curved knife in the room with all this stuff," I said to her, "I think its what he uses to make the cuts on his victims. It's probably crucial and it's gone."

"Maybe you forgot or it fell out..."

"I didn't forget. It didn't fall out. Someone took it."

Arlan began making a clicking sound. Several at the same time. I looked over, and he was both clicking his tongue and tapping his fingers on the glass-topped table at a speed just south of hummingbird.

"Chalice of flesh runneth over... world becomes the chalice—" he mumbled, then lifted his head and looked me dead in the eyes. He said, "This is a spell. This is a world-altering spell. I knew this was coming."

"You know what this is?" I leaned in to better study his face.

"Not this exactly, but one very like it. An old spell. And I know what time it is, cosmically speaking. And I know what people are capable of."

"Would you mind filling the rest of us in?"

"The world," Arlan said straightening to address the room, "the solar system and the galaxy we live in go through cycles. If my calculations are correct, once every two-thousand-three-hundred years or so, the world suffers a shift."

"Yeah, we got all that end-of-the-world crap in 2012," I said.

"No," he said, "This is different. What I'm referring to is a sort of reality shift. Remember the dark ages? Remember the witchcraft scare? If my theory is correct then that was the last cycle. The stories of vampires, werewolves, and the like. The pre-classical period before that with their animal-headed gods? Probably another cycle. All of our monster stories from primordial times, likely were due in part to this shift, and the fluctuation of magical energy into and out of reality."

"Are you fucking kidding me?" I wasn't quite shouting, but I wanted to. "People are dying, and you're going to stand here theorizing about *magic*? We need answers, not fairy tale horseshit."

Arlan just shrugged, unperturbed by my anger, "Quasi-religious cults all over the world are founded on the recorded lore from those times."

Unbelieving, I looked over at Toni, who was similarly aghast. Then I looked at Dr. Pape, also unperturbed. She caught my gaze out of the corner of her eye and looked up from the file.

"That is why Arlan is here," she said without missing a beat, "to be our folklorist."

"Folklorist!"

"Among other things. Some, if not all of the things that we deal with, like the recent six-legged lizard that could paralyze, have striking parallels with creatures and events from our own lore and legend. The theory Arlan has proposed seems plausible in the light of these recent developments, so yes. He's our folklorist."

"This is all horseshit." I was too exhausted to get properly pissed, "We need to get this guy, and we're looking into fairy tales."

"We will get him," Toni said, "After you rest up. Sandra—I mean Dr. Pape— just thought you should be brought up to speed."

"Nice. We couldn't have done this before people died?"

"People have been dying all along," Arlan countered, "The spell takes sacrifices to get the ball rolling. There is no telling how many were killed before we even became aware of something happening."

"It's what I was trying to tell you back in Maryland," Toni said, "The whole cryptid-lore-spells thing."

"Oh," I sighed, "Really? I just thought that was—really?"

They were all nodding at me, and suddenly it felt like I'd been running on empty for a really long time. As soon as it all started coming together in my head, I was so tired I couldn't stand, so I pulled a chair out and sat in it until the others were done talking and we were released to our rooms.

SIXTEEN

"The knife's not crucial," Toni was telling me over our early breakfasts in the lounge, "The other stuff is more than enough to put Hurt away for the bombing alone. Dead or alive this guy has got to be brought in. Now we just have to go get him."

"I hope I'm on that roster."

"Max, you've done enough."

"I want Hurt. I want him to know he didn't get to me. I want him to know it was me that put his ass down. I want to look him in his bony-ass face and tell him Therin's still alive." What I didn't say was how much I wanted to be the one to feel the old bastard's pulse stop under my own hands as they closed around his scrawny neck.

"Do you think that's wise?"

"I think it's necessary. He needs to know he can't spread his delusion to other people. That he's just fucking nuts and then he needs to pay for what he's done."

"We'll see what Dr. Pape says."

"Get me on it. Please."

Toni blushed. It was fetching on her. I felt myself blush a little too, but there was no time for those thoughts, those memories. There was only time to stop Hurt, and maybe not enough of that. I excused myself and went back to the breakfast bar to retrieve another blueberry muffin and a juice. Then, just for good measure, I got a new plate and filled it with eggs, sausage, bacon, biscuits, gravy and fruit. The truck stop seemed like forever ago, and I hadn't had much of an appetite in the hospital. It all came screaming back now.

When I returned to the table, Dr. Pape and Arlan were just coming around the corner, her with a cup of her usual black coffee and him with some weird-smelling tea. At least now I'd be able to take a shower since the old man was out. The thought of Arlan's shower singing, made me cringe. It was still early for the meeting room, so they joined us in the lounge.

Everyone was seated but me, so the sound of approaching high heels behind me, and the strange angry-fast pace of the sound made me want to duck for no reason I can rationally explain. Instead of embarrassing myself, though, I just clenched my jaw and turned to see who was coming. Just in time to get slapped in the face.

I backed up instinctively, knocking over the chair I would have occupied. Most women I sort of tower over, but not this one. In those deadly-looking gold heels, she was actually taller than me, and that dark hair in the topknot only added to the effect. Just as I was trying to remember her name, her leopard-print mini dress jerked, and she slapped me again. This time I caught her elbow.

"What the hell was that for?" I asked her as I tugged her away from the tableful of colleagues now behind me.

"You asked me three days ago to meet you back at your hotel room and you never showed. I lost two tricks that night because of you!"

"Patricia, I..."

"I don't want to hear it. We're done. Well, we never got properly started did we? I hope this lets your little girlfriend—or is she your wife—see just what kind of jackass you really are."

"They're my coworkers," I said, my ears on fire.

"Well, I hope you get fired. I got beat up because of you."

"No, I said, suddenly angry, "You got beat up because you chose to be a hooker with a pimp. Now get out of here before I have my boss call security."

"I ain't scared of your boss. Or security. You owe me three hundred bucks."

"You really need to leave, there's no payday for you here."

"We'll see," she said, pushing past me and walking right up to the table occupied by Dr. Pape—and Toni. "This guy hired me for a night and didn't show. I waited two hours, in which I could have made two-hundred bucks. He owes me and won't pay. Somebody want to cough it up or do I start screaming?"

There was a momentary pause during which everybody kind of held their breath. Toni was red as a beet, but Dr. Pape rose to Particia's challenge.

"Here's the three hundred. I am sure it will never happen again. In the meantime, might I suggest that it isn't a good idea to proposition government workers? As far as I can recollect, prostitution is still illegal in Oklahoma. Also, it does seem like the decision to wait for two hours on a potential client was a bad decision on your part, and that choosing not to partake of your services was a good one on his."

Patricia huffed, took the money and cast me a scathing glare as she strode back out. My ears were still burning when I sat back down at the table. I pushed the plate away, no longer hungry and only raised my eyes enough to glance at Toni's face. She did her best to keep it neutral, but there were traces of something there. Pity? Disappointment?

Dr. Pape broke the awkward silence. "So today we storm the castle. We're taking down Hurt Industries. I have Max leading the front team into the building, and Toni coordinating with local law enforcement and the FBI for a back team."

I looked back over at Toni and mouthed the word "Thanks", and she mouthed back, "Wasn't me", which made me curious. I kept silent though as Dr. Pape gave us a quick rundown on our strategy for taking the building. Now that Therin was under armed guard, I felt pretty good about taking the direct approach.

After her spiel, Pape said she'd meet us back in the meeting room, and I decided to go hit that shower. Suddenly I missed my duffel. As we walked to the elevators, I was finally able to talk to Toni.

"So, my duffel was in the Jeep when it disappeared. You think we might have some spare clothes somewhere?"

"I think there are some uniforms in one of the trucks. What happened to the Jeep?"

"Hurt probably had it towed. There's no telling if the duffel's been taken, and there were samples in there."

"We'll find it. I'll have someone call around to the yards. Max—"

"I am sorry Toni—about earlier. But I really don't want to talk about it, okay?"

"Sure," she said, her usual brusque manner returning somewhat. "I'll send up some clothes." She stalked off down the hall as the elevator doors slid open. Man, did I always have to be a heel?

There was a knock at the door as I showered, and I heard Arlan open it. Then it closed, and I heard him open the bathroom door.

"Here are your clothes," he called. Then the bathroom door closed again, and I heard him go out the room door. I supposed I had pretty much pissed everyone off this morning. What a great way to start a mission.

Once dressed, I headed back down to the meeting room. It did feel good to have a tee shirt on again. The fatigue pants were another story, but they'd have to do. Kai was there when I came in, and Toni. Both of them were dressed in the same gear and Toni's voluminous red curls were tucked into a neat bun at the nape of her neck. Arlan was dressed in his usual gaudy attire. The security guys were there, as well as people in various public service and government regulation uniforms.

Blueprints lay across the table and though I normally would have found a corner to listen from, I was taking point on this one and couldn't afford to be a wallflower.

I strode to the table, bumped the SWAT guy from his spot and stood at the end opposite Dr. Pape. The SWAT guy didn't look pleased, but moved to the side of the table without argument. Once Dr Pape acknowledged my arrival, all of the buzz in the room came to a halt. I had their full attention.

"The target is cunning, has a thing for traps and has a big time advantage on us," I said, "He isn't afraid to use unconventional means to get people out of his way, and you might encounter any number of diversion tactics. He likes to mess with people's minds. Mind-altering substances are not out of the question. If you see something you can't explain, try not to panic. Work in pairs, and send a team through every accessible entrance."

I looked over the blueprints briefly before continuing. "When you go in, detain everyone, lock It down. Arrest everyone that looks vaguely henchman-like. Hold the rest until we get an idea of who all is involved. I want shooters on the surrounding buildings, covering the exits and the windows as far up as we can go. This man has a plan for genocide. Take the shot if you get one." I looked at Dr. Pape, and she nodded gravely.

"I also want a chopper up there, to cover the places we can't reach and to set me on the roof. I want to make sure that bastard can't take off in a bird of his own. Whatever he's planning, it's worldwide, and that's no bueno for the US if it happens. That makes this a matter of national security, for real. This is not a drill." There were nods around the table, except for the SWAT guy.

"Why isn't the military taking care of this if it's a matter of national security? I mean, I've never even heard of you people until today. My commander says follow orders and I will, but it'd be nice to know whose orders they really are."

"They're mine. They're yours. They belong to every human being on the face of this planet that doesn't want to die in whatever hell this guy wants to unleash. Is that good enough for you?"

"Yeah." The guy swallowed a bit. "It'll do."

I rolled up the blueprints and handed them off to SWAT guy. "What was your name?"

"Thomas. Vince Thomas."

"Well Vince. Let's go save the world."

With that I bugged out of the meeting room. I did the pep talk, now I had to breathe. *Save the world? What the hell was I thinking?* My chest was aching vaguely again, and I leaned against the hallway wall beside the door, listening to the muffled conversations behind me.

The door opened. Toni stepped into the hall. She stopped in front of me and laid a hand on my shoulder. I must have looked shaken, because she met my eyes evenly, evaluating.

"You okay?" Then a moment later she said, "No. What is it?"

"Nothing."

"Liar," she said, stepping closer, "Tell me." Her voice was soft, and she was entirely too close. There was no time for this.

"Toni," I said, taking a deep breath which, filled as it was with her scent, didn't help, "I can't do this now. We need to get rolling. This needs to get done."

"If you're not mission-ready..."

"I'm ready," I said, looking away, "I'm not the one holding this thing up."

"Max..." Her hand slid down my arm, and I felt like my chest was going to implode.

"You really need to stop talking now." I gathered her up, pulling her tight against me. I kissed her. I knew it was wrong and I didn't care. If we were going to die—if she was going to die, at least she'd know. The pain in my chest was worse, but I felt better anyway. I waited for her to pull away and slap me, but she didn't. She kissed me back, her lips hot on mine, swollen from the suddenness of the first kiss.

I took a ragged breath and whispered, "You don't get anywhere near this thing." She did step back then, and regarded me exactly as if nothing had happened.

"I have a job to do, and I intend to do it."

"People die on my watch. I don't want you to be one of them."

"It'll take more than your "bad juju" to make me dead, Maxwell Edison," she said coolly, "I do not require your protection."

I thought about the morning she'd put me on my ass in hand-to-hand and knew that, of course, she didn't need my protection. She didn't need me at all. We'd been through so much, but she'd never been just one of the guys. Nor could she be with me. The work was too important.

The door opened again and we stood apart. Dr. Pape was the first out of the room. She appeared to make a mental note of our appearance, and then simply passed by. We fell in step behind her, followed by the rest of the assemblage.

Her radio squawked and Dr. Pape called back "Our vehicles are ready. Call out your teams and let's go get the son-of-a-bitch."

Toni and I glanced at each other. Dr. Pape didn't cuss.

SEVENTEEN

I was uneasy in the helo seat. I'd never been a big fan of things that defied the laws of physics. It's sort of how I wound up in this job. That and jobs were scarce after the war. Things looked pretty quiet as we neared the building. Traffic had been fairly calm and unperturbed until the ground teams began to set up their perimeter. Once the entry teams were at the entrance, I signaled the pilot to take him in. The chopper hovered over the roof as the tech got me strapped into the harness and lowered me down to the roof.

Once the buffeting of the chopper blades faded and the roaring in my ears eased up, I could hear the chatter in my earpiece. Toni's order came through, and I tried the door to the stairwell. Finding it locked, I fed it a couple of rounds and gave it a good yank to let the lock pieces fall out and the door swing open. I took the short flight of stairs down to the penthouse office. While I was going I heard the scattered shots and shouting of the SWAT guys making their initial entry. Then things settled, and as I entered the office itself, the only thing over the headset was the usual chatter of offices, rooms and floors being systematically cleared and contained. The penthouse office seemed to be empty.

I made my way to the desk, being careful to look for tripwires, trapdoors, and other nefarious devices my host might have lying in wait. Though I found none, I was still leery as I opened the top desk drawer. The only thing there was an envelope with my name on it. I tore it open and scanned the contents.

There was a picture of Therin in her hospital bed and a note that read, "Already arranged for the cleaning lady. I hope you don't mind. There was nothing you could have done, anyway."

Other than the envelope, the office was completely empty. No computer, no files, nothing. I stuffed the envelope and its former contents into one of the cargo pockets of the fatigue pants and looked around the room again.

People had identified Hurt coming into the office that morning, and no one had said that he left. I tapped the button on my headset and said, "Can we confirm that Hurt is still in the building? Did anyone see him leave?"

"Confirmed," Toni said, "No one has seen him leave. The lower levels are secured."

"Check the video from this morning. He's not in his office."

"Will do."

There was silence, except for static and the occasional check-in as they continued to secure levels. So far I'd heard from all the lower levels except the basement. Losing my fear of traps, in favor of the fear of coming up empty-handed, I went all around the office, opening everything that would open. The little restroom was empty, as was the little den area with the fake fireplace. These had been on the blueprints and were along the outer wall.

I considered the central elevator and stairwell. That's when it hit me. The tower hadn't been dancing when we got there. That alcove on the blueprints that ran through all the floors along the elevator shaft, I'd figured was ventilation. Looking now at the area beside the elevator, all I could see was a wet bar.

"We have a problem in the basement, folks." It was Vince's voice.

"Did you find him?" Toni's voice.

"No ma'am. But this building's rigged to come down, and it won't be pretty."

"Evacuate immediately." Toni's voice. "Get everyone out of here right now. We'll worry about questioning later."

"It looks like a demolitions setup," Vince's voice said, "Multiple charges, but no timer though."

"I hate to ask," I said into the headset, "but can you all look at the wall by the elevator shaft for your floor? Do you see anything?"

"Negative on four."

"Nothin' on seven."

"Good, you guys get out of here."

"That means you too, Max," Toni's voice ordered.

"Be right there." I lied. I tried all the doors, and found no switches, no buttons, nothing. Finally, having a "Young Frankenstein" flashback, I pulled all the bottles out of the wine rack, one by one. The very last bottle on the bottom right resisted.

I felt a wicked grin cross my face, and said to myself, "I'm taking the express down."

I pulled hard, and the bottle finally gave, releasing a catch behind the bar. The whole mirror-backed affair swung out and revealed the small elevator doors and the button panel. There was only one outer button, so I pressed it. There was a trundling sound and soon the doors hissed open. I got in and noted that there were only two buttons here. Up and down. I pushed the down button.

I thought I'd been kidding about the express part, but the doors closed silently and the small box dropped pretty swiftly. The box slowed and the doors opened to reveal a brand new but still dank-looking tunnel. There were no readouts in the elevator, so I had no way of knowing how far down I'd gone. I was really starting to hate tunnels.

At least this tunnel didn't have leaping lampreys or tentacle terrors that I could tell. Still, I led with my weapon as I cautiously exited the elevator. There was a knot in my stomach. This didn't feel right. I began to wonder if Hurt had ever really come in at all. Still, I had to hope I was right behind the guy. That I was following him away from the building and therefore away from any possible detonation. Toni deserved a better goodbye than a kiss in a hallway. Better than a lie on a headset. Now that I thought about it, I didn't want to say goodbye. It was wrong, but she got me. And Gods, did she look glorious when she blushed. I wanted to see her blush again.

The tunnel was long, and got darker the further down I went. There weren't any offshoots, and there was no loud boom. I wondered if they'd disarmed the explosives. The more steps I took, the narrower the tunnel got and the more uneasy I got. Just when I got to the point where the walls were brushing my shoulders, I felt the jolt and heard the boom. Actually it was only the first part of the explosion that I heard. After that I was senseless, enveloped in darkness. I wasn't unconscious, but I was deafened by the blast, and the dark was complete. I'd been knocked off my feet by the concussion, but I didn't feel hurt.

I patted my pockets to find the new phone Dr. Pape had insisted I carry, and with its small light, I was able to make out some of my surroundings for a few feet in either direction. It was enough for me to see that the tunnel had collapsed behind me. Like two feet behind me. *If I had hesitated any longer coming out of that elevator—Toni did you get out?* There was no time for prayers or mourning now. I scrambled to my feet and pressed on down the shrinking tunnel. There was nowhere else to go, anyway.

Finally, when I had to turn sideways, and tilt my head to advance, I came to a door. Feeling a bit like Alice after she partook of the local refreshments, I opened the little door, and ducked under the frame into the adjacent room. Except there was no room. The blinding brightness that forced me to shut my eyes was sunlight. The door opened into the great outdoors. I was in a park. Still downtown, but I had to be blocks away from the tower.

My headset crackled to life as soon as I stepped out, but my hearing was shot. I could barely hear Toni's voice, tight, asking if anyone had seen me. When the returning reports all said no, she said, "Keep looking."

"I don't know where I am," I said simply.

"Max!" Her shout would have hurt if I wasn't already partially deaf.

"Yeah, I'm in a park. Can you honk or something so I can find you?" Then, as I was looking up, I spun around and saw the smoke drifting from the building. "Never mind. I see it. Hurt's in the wind."

"Thank God, you made it."

"God had exactly shit to do with it." I ripped the headset off and let it dangle around my neck as I stalked back to help with whatever I could. There were more injured than we could count, but the fatalities were few. There were maybe half a dozen office workers unaccounted for, and the four in our basement crew. Vince was among them. There was damage to almost every building in a three-block radius; and there were innumerable injuries to random people on the street from projectiles and smoke. Vince had been right. It wasn't pretty.

EIGHTEEN

I flung open the hotel room door and flung my gear into the room as hard as I could. Arlan, who had been right behind me decided that it would be a good idea to go and address one more thing with Dr. Pape down the hall. I undressed and hit the head and then was already in the shower before I realized that the only clothes I had were the ones I'd just taken off and the ones I'd worn through the sewer a few days ago.

When I got out, I wrapped a towel around my waist and draped one around my neck. Then I sat at the little desk and called room service. As the phone rang I looked up and caught the reflection of my blond head in the television screen and thought about Therin. *Poor kid. Sounds like wine for dinner. A bottle. Maybe two. Make it three and it'll feel like payday.*

When the room service guy told me they didn't serve wine before five pm, I had a sudden urge to hit something, but felt silly getting all pissed off in a towel, so I just asked him if they had a laundry. He said they did, and that it was on the first floor between the gym and the pool room. *Can we really afford this place?* Ultimately it didn't matter.

If Hurt was really unstoppable, and it was certainly looking like he might be, then The Office of Human Protection had failed utterly, and would cease to exist, or Pape would blame the failure on a lack of funding and governmental support and they'd have all the backing they'd need. I could only think of one thing that might even up the odds a little.

There was only one way to fight magic (if that was really what this was) this potent. I gathered up both sets of clothes, wrapped them in a third towel, then grabbed my wallet and key card and headed for the laundry. I could only hope I happened across Toni in a deserted hallway again.

***

Once my clothes were clean and I was dressed in my own slacks and the clean tee shirt from yesterday, I picked up the phone and dialed. This time it wasn't room service I called. There was one more thing I had to do before I got shitfaced. I called a cab. Then I used the cell phone to call home.

"Edison residence. This is Vierna."

"Mama?"

"Max," she said it long and loud, and I could feel the warmth of her joy in her drawl.
She'd be smiling on the other end.

My godmother let out a big deep laugh of sheer delight at the thought that her boy had called her.

"How are you sweetnin'? No. Wait. Oh I am so sorry dear child. Tell mama about it." The sound of her smile was gone.

I tried to draw a breath to begin, but my throat threatened to close on me. "I can't, Mama. I need help. We all do. I need the Lwa."

"No child. I told you. They're not for you. The Lwa would make something else of you. Maybe better, maybe worse, but not the same. You have a different magic."

"I don't have any magic."

"Of course you do. You just don't think it *is* magic. Don't worry though, the Lwa are already sensing what is happening and will handle it in their own way."

"What way is that? Dancing and spewing chicken blood everywhere? Mama, I need real help."

"Your help will come, child but it will be too late. You cannot stop what is to come. Nobody can."

"Are you drinking the same Kool-Aid as the guy I'm chasing? That's the same exact thing he said."

"No, Maxwell. You know very well what I do and how I know what I know. Now, I can make a gris-gris for you, but that is all. No Lwa. No conjure. Baron Samedi is already astride his horse and will not come to such as us. He is getting ready for the great gathering in."

"There has to be something."

"This thing you called about. It is so much bigger than you. Please, find a place to be safe until it is over. I will make gris-gris to help protect you, but I do not know if you will thank me for it or not." She took a deep breath and then her spirit-voice took over saying,

"Dark times comin'—Down come the countin' house— Dark times comin'." And then her regular voice came over the line again saying, "The bone sliver gotta come out before the moon turns full."

"Okay. Look, If you can't help I have to go."

"You having seen all you seen, and you still want to act like you don't believe. You gonna believe when it happens, boy. Everybody's gonna believe."

"Nothing's going to happen because I'm going to stop it. I can't just let this guy walk."

"He's not going to walk. He's going to die. You're gonna kill him and it still won't stop what's to happen. It ain't got hardly anything to do with him hisself."

"Be careful Mama, I love you."

"I love you too, child."

"Bye."

"Goodbye," she said, and she hung up.

Mama Vierna never said goodbye. At least I was going to get to kill the sonofabitch. Vierna was infamously vague with her predictions at the best of times, but this one was different. This time I knew what was coming—sort of. Then there was the knowledge she seemed to have about things he hadn't mentioned, and her prediction about him killing Hurt was very direct. What baffled me most, though, was the part about the bone sliver. As far as she knew they'd got all the pieces before. Hell, I'd only found out days ago, and hadn't breathed a word to anyone.

I walked out of the hotel room and downstairs to the front doors. It was raining again. *October in Oklahoma. Yay.* The cab pulled up and I got in. I still hadn't heard anything about the Jeep or my duffel.

"Impound yard please, and the quicker the better." It was time to get my shit back if it was still there.

As it turned out, the Jeep had been impounded and my duffel was in the back seat. I used the Office card to pay the fees and called the rental company. I extended my rental, putting it on a weekly turnover with the card and then, retrieving the new key from the impound guy, I got in it and drove it back to the hotel. Fuck room service. Fuck wine. I had rum.

***

"Okay," Dr. Pape said. "Our guy is in the wind. Where does a billionaire go when he's on the run?"

"The islands," Toni said.

"Switzerland," somebody behind me offered.

"The NSA has grounded all flights into and out of Tulsa until we get our guy. We've lost jurisdiction on this rat. He's on the news. He's officially a terrorist."

"I'll get on NSA collaboration," Toni said, ducking out of the room.

"Arlan, I want you to tell me you've found something on this 'chalice of flesh' thing and the spell that's attached to it."

"Sadly, the only thing I have been able to find on the chalice of flesh is a correlation between it and the end of the world. I believe it is Late-Norse or Gaelic in origin, but without my original texts from home, I can't be sure which." I finally pinned down that accent. It was English. Northern, but apparently he'd been in the states a long time, because it was faint.

"Max," she said, turning her attention to me, "I need for you to disappear for a while. Get off the radar. Find this bastard and stay out of the NSA's way. Keep in touch, and we'll relay any info we get."

"Will do."

"And Max," she said, a glint of mischief in her eye, " Stay out of tunnels."

"We'll see," I said, giving her a wink. Pape was alright. The NSA—not so much.

I figured I'd start by checking up on Therin. Despite their promises, I'd had no word on how she was doing through all the chaos. At the hospital, I took the stairs, double time, up the two floors to her room. She was in a regular room now, and when I swung the door open she was sitting up, but still looked like hell. She saw me and grinned broadly.

"Max! Oh, my god, I was so worried when they said Hurt Tower blew up! I could hear the boom from here! I thought he got you!"

"He tried. Again. How are you?"

"They say I'm doing fine, they just want to keep me a couple of days longer to make sure everything's healing right and I won't pull the sutures. I'll get out just in time for school to start back up. Great fall break, huh?"

"Well I can't stay. I just wanted to get eyes on you. I should have brought you flowers or something."

"Nah. Flowers are for girly-girls. You could bring me a cheeseburger, though. With everything. And some fries. *That* would be great."

"Consider it done." As soon as the words left my mouth, my heart sank. "I don't know how soon I'll be able to get that here though. Hurt got away."

"Yeah. That was on the news too. Max, will you please be careful?"

"I'm always careful," I said, sensing the worry in her tone. Then I gave her a wink and said, "It's not my fault it doesn't help. Gotta go." I started for the door, but her voice stopped me again.

"Max," she said, "Thanks for saving my life."

"It was my fault you were down there. And besides, you saved me too."

"Seriously. Thank you."

"No mushy stuff." I said, then in a moment of sudden feeling, I said. "Thank you, too."

I ducked out the door and strode down the hallway. As I walked I looked up the number for Kane Quinn, bounty hunter. There were some explanations in order. I got in the elevator and tapped the call button on the screen. Somehow I'd thought he'd be harder to find.

"Quinn Bail Bonds, Winter, what can I do ya for?" What I wanted to say was "free", but I wasn't sure who I was dealing with yet.

"I'd like to make an appointment with Kane Quinn," was what actually came out of my mouth.

"Kane Quinn don't take appointments, but he's not here right now anyhow. Can I take your number and have him call you when he gets in?"

"He can return the call to this number, and tell him it's the guy he gave a ride to the other day."

"Kane gave you a ride? I—mean sure. I'll let him know."
She hung up.

"Now there's a professional," I said to no one in
particular.

I was so sure Hurt was going to show himself again
before the big—whatever, that I decided to find a bar. A real
bar, and not that lounge back at the hotel. I found one,
conveniently across the street from the hotel, so I parked in
the hotel parking lot and walked across. They might get me for
public drunk, but I wouldn't be behind the wheel.

I thought about going up to see if Toni wanted to come,
but decided against it. Just me and Patron tonight. With the
NSA boys sniffing around, I was better off out of sight and out
of mind.

I grabbed a stool and ordered my first shot, and a beer
to chase it with. I downed the shot and then almost spewed it
back in the barkeep's face when someone clapped a hand on
my shoulder. I turned to see who needed the shit kicked out of
them. It was Quinn. *Ah well I wasn't much in the shit-kicking
mood anyway.* I took a pull off my beer.

"I see you got my message."

"Yeah, you're way too easy to track slick. Next time
maybe try a hat or something."

"I wasn't hiding. Not from you anyway. You want a
beer?"

"No, I'm still working. Just stopped here while I was on this side of town. What was it you wanted?"

I turned to regard the man. His manner seemed easy enough, but there was something about him that made me uneasy. Something wasn't right. Maybe it was just the bounty hunter thing. It gave people a predatory look.

"The pack I gave you. Did you open it?"

"No, why?"

"Something was missing when it got to my boss, and I'm just trying to track it down. It's pretty much only you and one other guy that had contact with it."

"Well Hoss, I suggest you ask the other guy. I don't steal nothing without a damn good reason."

"That's kind of what I was thinking too. If you were to have a damn good reason, what might it be? Then I got to thinking how convenient it was you being right there when Therin and I needed a ride to the hospital."

"Look Jackpot Junior, I don't have your whatsit. If the pack was opened, it was after I handed it off."

"Never mind. It wasn't you."

"Damn straight it wasn't. Want me to wring the little turd's neck?"

"No," I said, "But there is something you might could do to help."

Quinn eyed me sideways and said, "Well, shit the bed. You want me to help you after you accuse me of stealing?"

"I wasn't accusing, just asking. Accusing is much more violent."

"Now you're threatening me?"

"You feel threatened?"

"No. Punk."

"I'm explaining."

"Okay. What is it?"

"You ever tracked a terrorist?"

"Fuck."

NINETEEN

Long after Quinn went off to do whatever the hell Quinn did, I was still sitting at the bar sucking down beer. They cut me off at about ten and I sat there glaring at the television that was showing continuous coverage of my mistakes. I'd failed to get this guy in hand not once or twice, but three times now. Twenty-two was the final death toll from the blast alone. Seven of them Office, and another was Vince. Hurt had known we were coming. The knife had disappeared. *If Kai took the knife...*

I left the bar so fast my bar stool was still spinning when I hit the door. I ran back across the street, thankful it was a Thursday. I ran up the stairs and beat on Toni's room door. When she opened it, it was clear she'd been sleeping, but that didn't matter now.

"Where's Kai?"

"Max? It's late. Are you drunk?"

"Sorta. Where is he?"

"How the hell should I know?"

"Because you liaise. That's like being an overpaid dispatcher, right? So where'd you send him?"

"I don't know Max," she said, glaring at me. "It's not like I keep all that shit in my head. Ask me in the morning when you're not drunk."

"If I don't get him now, he'll get away. I've already screwed this up too much. Kai's our mole."

"What?"

"Kai. He's our mole. He's working with Hurt." Now that I'd said it, it wasn't just mine. Toni would bear some of the responsibility too.

"That's crazy, Kai's your friend. Besides, he's been a faithful agent for years."

"Was. Now he's committing treason. Against all of humanity."

"What makes you think so?"

"He was the only one other than Quinn to have possession of the pack when the knife went missing. That and the look on his face when he saw that it was me you were picking up at the hospital. I thought it was—nostalgia. It was guilt. He was there when we were planning the raid yesterday morning. It's Kai."

"Hang on," she said, undoing the chain across the door to let me in, "Be quiet. Dr. Pape's sleeping."

"Anyone ever just call her Sandra?"

"I almost did the other day, but it didn't feel right. I don't think anyone's willing to risk it. The sky might fall. Here, I have everyone's info on my laptop."

"Is that safe?"

"It is on this laptop." She flipped open the little computer and started hitting the keys so fast it made me a little queasy. I don't think I could have kept up with her keystrokes sober. That was why she got the big bucks.

"Okay," she said, "I've got him. He's staking out one of Hurt's favorite nightclubs."

"Let me guess. The Cain's."

"No," she said, and I thought I was going to fall over, "Technically that's a concert hall. This is a tiny little place over on Fifteenth. The Cherry Street Bar and Grill."

"I'm on it."

"No, you're not."

"The hell?"

"You're almost too drunk to stand. Go to bed. I'll get someone else to bring him in."

"I can't just…"

"Maxwell Edison, if you try to leave this hotel again tonight, I'll have you arrested before you can even get to the door."

I didn't reply, but gave her what I hoped was a very hurt look, and slunk out the door and down the hall to my room. There was no way she was going to let me get back out, and I'd get a shot at Kai sooner or later. At least in theory. For now, that was going to have to do it. I was getting awful sleepy.

Arlan was singing in the shower when I opened the door, and I flopped on the little couch. I wondered for a moment if everyone I worked with was plotting to undo me. I pushed that thought away, and another rushed in behind it. *Can I even trust Toni?* I pushed that one away as well, and when I looked up a towel-wrapped, steaming Arlan stood in the bathroom doorway smiling at me. I'd been wondering if he partook. Now was as good a time as any to find out.

"Arlan, old buddy," I grinned, "How about we split a bottle of wine?"

He gave me a long look, but then brightened and asked, "Red or white?"

"Red," I said, "and the stronger the better." Arlan ordered the wine, went to put on clothes and then came back and sat in the overstuffed chair across the coffee table from me.

"You want to know about the spell, don't you?"

"Of course, doesn't everybody?"

"Yes, but you are in a unique position. You could hold the key to whether it comes to complete fruition or not."

"You sound like Vierna. I don't have any keys, Arlan. And I don't have any magic. Or answers, and I fail at everything I do."

"No, dear boy," he said. "You never fail until you quit or until you're dead."

"Thanks for the cheering up."

He pshawed and then said, "I can help you understand, and you and the other agents can act where I cannot."

"You said you hadn't found anything on the chalice of flesh."

"Indeed, I haven't. I do, however, know a little about spells in general. I'm signed on with The Office to teach you all such things. Would you like to start now?"

"I'm afraid I won't remember much of it in the morning."

"Now that is something I can do something about." Arlan cracked his knuckles like a caricature of a concert pianist and went back into the bedroom. He returned with a small vial and held it up for me to take.

"Drink this before we talk and it will help you remember everything we talk about no matter how much you drink."

"Dare I ask?"

"Best not. Bottoms up."

"Damn." I unstopped the vial and pressed it against my lips. Then I tipped my head back to let the liquid pour down my throat. It was warm and sweet like a wine itself. When I drank it, the buzz I'd spent all night cultivating began to fade. By the time the actual wine arrived, I was stone sober and a little pissy.

Arlan poured the wine and observed me from beneath his bushy gray eyebrows. "I hope it is the taste of wine you like, as drinking it will have no effect on you for the rest of the night."

"That's a dirty trick to play on a guy."

"For your own good, I'm afraid. Now, where do we start?"

"I guess at the beginning."

"No, that was too long ago. Let's just go back to ten-thousand or so BCE. That should get us there a lot faster." I nodded for him to continue, but was having serious reservations about his ability to convince me that he knew anything about ten-thousand BCE.

"The idea that man has the ability to affect nearly instantaneous change in the world around him is nearly as old as man itself. These unquantifiable ideas, prayer or magic, are only considered fiction because of a carefully orchestrated sociopolitical construct based on purely repeatable and consistent empirical data called science."

"But magic doesn't work."

"You are sober, yes?"

"Unfortunately. But that was some kind of herbal junk, right? That was science. Chemicals."

"Of course, but it was also enchanted." Arlan's eyes were twinkling as he reclined back into the chair. "It shouldn't work, but it does. Well, it does now, anyway. That is how I know I'm on the right track with my observations. Actually magic has always worked a little bit, just not enough to easily quantify and reliably replicate."

"Wow. Okay, say I buy into all of this. Why? Why is it so much stronger, this spell?"

"Because someone found a way to work just a little magic at the right time in history. A way to work magic without magic being strong in the world, but at just the right moment for that door to be ready to open. A way to birth magic back into the world on a grand scale. It likely took them a very long time to build the energy up to this level. Unless this is stopped, it will keep feeding back into itself and the waves will just continue. The entire world will change."

"There is someone out there able to make magic without magic? I'm pretty open minded, since I was raised by Mama Vierna, but I don't know if I buy that one person could do all this."

"As I was saying earlier, it is likely several people."

"This Shadow Council."

"They do seem the likeliest candidates. Also the basic hypothesis is that this cycle happens semi-regularly. This time, it's getting a rocket boost."

"Okay," I said, considering another sip of wine and then deciding it wasn't worth it, "so with all your insight, what would it take—if you were to do something like this—what would it take to make it happen?"

"First, I'd need those helpers. Then I'd have to get the timing just right. Then I'd need sacrifices at a specific set of ritual sites, and a sort of central hidden site at which the larger spell would be initiated. In short, I'd have to establish a network."

"So all I'd have to do to stop it would be to find this central site and destroy it?"

"Absolutely not. In fact that may be the worst thing you could do. There will be redundancies, but if you throw it off, the results could be worse than the initial spell."

"So it's hopeless then?" I went for the wine, and instead of a sip, I downed it. Maybe it was a volume thing.

"There is always hope. Would you like to know what you can do right now to help?"

"Of course. That's kind of what it's all about, isn't it?"

""Of course," Arlan said, then he stood and went to the bedroom again. There was a zipping sound and some shuffling, and then he returned with a long stem pipe and a leather pouch.

He resumed his position in the chair and opened the pouch. A sweet, almost licorice smell rose to meet my nose. We both inhaled deeply. The smell of the stuff made me feel all warm and tingly, and reminded me a little of the stuff he had me drink. I was suddenly wary.

"That doesn't smell like pot. Doesn't smell like tobacco either."

"Oh, this is not that. Not even close. This is about as close to cannabis as cannabis is to alfalfa. This is a special blend, passed down through generations in my family. Just an old recipe from Europe." He packed the bowl of the pipe and lit it, taking a long luxurious draw of the sweet-smelling smoke. Then he offered me the pipe.

I didn't usually partake, but this little ritual of his might just help, and if there was even a remote possibility... I took the pipe and at first, just took a small pull. The smoke was smooth, and slightly relaxing.

"You're going to have to do better than that, son," Arlan said, smiling sympathetically. I let it out and took another draw, this one more like the one Arlan had taken.

"Now," Arlan said, taking the pipe carefully from my quickly relaxing hand, "Think only on your goal to help mitigate the damage from this spell."

"I don't want to mitigate. I want to stop it."

"Just focus on what you need to do right now for the best possible outcome."

I felt the same spinning sensation I got sometimes on the edge of sleep. The room was fading, but I didn't fight it. I allowed the darkness rising behind my eyes to envelop me, and everything ceased to be.

TWENTY

I found myself standing atop a seaside cliff beside an enormous, gnarled, leafless tree. Looking out across the gulf, I could just see a little village to my right along the shore below, and waves that grew more violent as I watched. Dark clouds seemed to billow from behind me and they soon loomed over the tiny village as well. The wind blew. It seemed to come from everywhere at once. Lightning lashed the sky in helter-skelter flashes.

There was a rumbling beneath me, and for a minute I thought I was going over the cliff, but I wound up on my ass instead. I stood back up and looked down at the village again. Then I looked back out at the sea. At a certain spot on the horizon, the horizon line itself seemed to bulge.

By the time I realized it was an enormous wave, there was no time to make it to the village. I turned to try anyway, but at that instant a lightning bolt struck the tree beside me. The tree exploded, knocking me down again. I scramble to my feet and just ran. I ran as fast as I could, the growling storm seeming to chase me with some evil intelligence. Then there was a blue-white flash, followed immediately by darkness.

The next thing I knew, I was walking with Therin. We were at a college campus. She was carrying a white paper bag under one arm and a phone in her hand. Then there was blood and the sound of a woman screaming. There was darkness and pain, and I could feel myself running again as if my life depended on it. I was more afraid than I'd ever been, and that included Afghanistan. This terror was after me. It would consume me. Running, running and then falling, rolling and scrambling to run again I thought my chest would explode.

A new scene opened before me. There was an open air stage—an amphitheater? And a woman—I didn't know her. There was a man—but not exactly a man, more like a werewolf. He had her pinned to the concrete stage. She fought with the beast, but he was so much bigger and stronger. She seemed to shine against the darkness of the beast. I lunged down toward her, I had to help. Instead of running down the steps, though, I seemed to fly from the top of the amphitheater. I floated a moment, and then this scene too faded. I was surrounded in darkness again.

When I came back to my sense, Arlan was pulling me to my feet. I could smell smoke, and it wasn't the smoke from the pipe.

"What the hell?"

"The hotel fire alarms are going off. We have to go."

I took my own weight and ducked into the bedroom to get my duffel. I spotted the unzipped bag Arlan had pulled the pipe from and grabbed that too.

"Please," Arlan was calling from the doorway, "Let's go. I'm an old man, and I don't move so fast."

"Grab that pipe! I've got the bags!" I followed Arlan out the door and down the stairs. I could hear Toni and Dr. Pape ahead of us somewhere, but couldn't see them through the smoke. The stairway was filling up fast, but we were all making good time. Arlan, of course, wasn't nearly as slow as he'd made out. We emerged in the lobby and were ushered toward the front doors.

Just as we got clear of the stairwell and started forward toward the exit, there was an explosion from somewhere inside. It wasn't anything like the Hurt Tower, but it was enough to scare the crap out of people, especially in light of recent events. The crowd surged forward and Arlan got shoved to the side in the crush. I stopped and stood as still as possible, Sometimes I had to step back and let someone around me. Inch by inch I was able to make my way to where Arlan was stuck at the edge of the crowd. The crush was worse here, and I had to push back pretty hard to get the last few paces.

I reached out an arm and anchored it against the wall, refusing to let anyone push through. Then I opened up a space under it that Arlan could duck into. Maybe it was the exertion, maybe it was the adrenaline, but my chest was starting to ache again and I was getting angry. Arlan ducked into the space I made him with my body, and we made our way to the door. I wasn't losing one more person.

Outside, I caught sight of Toni and Dr. Pape, and I steered Arlan in their direction. Toni followed us over with her gaze as I deposited Arlan and his bag beside them. Neither one of us said anything as I turned to go. She wouldn't understand, and she was better off away from me. I attracted bad shit like bad shit attracted flies. I lugged my duffel back to the Jeep and got in.

If I got out before the first responders arrived, I could make the hospital in twenty, and I wasn't leaving Therin's side until I knew she was safe. She'd been in my vision, and though I didn't see exactly what happened, with the blood and the screaming, it couldn't have been good. If she was supposed to be one of the sacrifices and if their choosing wasn't random, Hurt wouldn't quit until he got her. *Was she chosen for her abilities? She and Jack both had them, but what about Claire? There were obviously things she didn't tell me, but that?*

When I got to Therin's room, she was sleeping. No one was posted at her door. The nurse told me she was doing better, and that she'd probably be released in the morning. I didn't want to wake her, so I parked my ass on the bench outside and the next thing I knew I was snapping awake.

The nurse stood over me, shaking my shoulder. I sat up frowning severely at her through my bleary eyes. Hangovers were never this bad. I felt like I was going to hurl on her shoes.

Therin was awake and eating breakfast when I went in to see her. The smell of eggs made me queasy again, but I was glad to see her up and smiling. She'd been allowed to shower and looked refreshed.

"Hey you," I said, peering around the curtain.

"Hay Max! I'm losing this joint today." She looked me up and down, and tried to look around the curtain behind me. "You were supposed to bring me a ch—what happened?"

"They lit up the hotel I was at again. This time I think it was just supposed to be fire, but something went boom anyway." I sat on the edge of the bed at her feet. "I'm beginning to feel like I'm being pushed along. Like someone else is in charge and they've got it in for me. Like the whole world's under attack and maybe some of it is my fault."

"That's stupid."

"I know."

"It's getting nuts out there, but how the fuck are you supposed to do anything about it? You been watching the news?"

I shook my head.

"There's been shootings and the church guys are all 'book of Revelation' and there are all these sightings of monsters of all kinds. There have been all these hit and runs, stabbings, and things and a lot of the perps are saying that they were made to do them. Compelled. Kinda like you were talking about." She looked me over again, her eyes seeming to search mine.

"Therin," I said, hoping I looked as sober and serious as I felt, "they're probably not going to leave you alive if they can help it. You need to be in protective custody."

"What good is that going to do if it's the whole world? Shouldn't I be helping you find the guy responsible and stop this?"

"This might sound stupid, but I don't think Hurt is the top of this thing."

"Not really. He's powerful and rich, but he's not the smartest. My brother's smarter."

"I thought you said he was a druggie."

"He was. Past tense. And that was only so he could slow his brain down. It's like their curse or something. That's why they asked him to work undercover. We could use his help. And he would keep me as safe as anyone could."

"I fail to see how he could help us."

"He's only got a half-year until he finished his doctorate in microbiology."

I stared at her. She continued.

"Microbiology is the day job. Metaphysics is his real love, and he's got ideas about shit that will blow your mind. He's also got skills like mine. Well not exactly, he's just a regular telepath."

"Oh," I said. "Is your whole family...?" I bugged my eyes out and wiggled my fingers spookily.

Therin literally laughed out loud. It was a warm, full sound that reminded me of a daydream. "No silly, our stuff is new too, but he's had his longer than me. That's how he knew how to train me."

"How long?"

"He's had his about a year or so, he said."

The nurse came in. I'd lost all track of time. If Daniel was like Therin, maybe there were more altered people running around than we thought. Perhaps the reason Hurt was hunting them had nothing at all to do with drugs. If so, then Daniel would be in just as much danger as Therin. The nurse unhooked Therin's IV and turned off her monitor.

"Would you like another tray before you go?" the nurse asked her. "I think we have a couple extra."

"No thanks," Therin said, "I've got a date with a cheeseburger."

The nurse chuckled and I couldn't help grinning. Then she left and I went out to the hall so she could get dressed. A few minutes later, she emerged from the room and sat beside me on the little bench. She rocked a little and nudged me with her shoulder.

"Thanks," she said.

"No problem."

After about two hours of waiting for release papers, I was pretty anxious to get moving. This was no time to be cooling my heels. Maybe pulling rank wasn't such a horrid thing to do. I stalked to the nurse's station and flashed my badge, telling the nurse that time was of the essence as nicely as I could manage under the circumstances. Five minutes later we were walking out the door. Well, I was walking, and pushing Therin in her wheel chair. Despite it being the middle of the day, the brisk wind had turned even cooler, and the dark clouds looming overhead reminded me of those from the vision. I couldn't be sure if it was a thunderstorm forming or a snowstorm.

An orderly came out and stood with her while I went to get the Jeep. I pulled it up to the entry and the orderly wheeled her out and opened the door. She climbed up into the jeep and he shut the door behind her. She beamed at me.

"Where to?" It was all I could think of to say that wouldn't burden her with my dark thoughts. I had a funky feeling in the guts that really made me want to leave her in the hospital.

"I've got to get something good in my stomach before I die of blandness or starve to death."

"Yeah. Are you sure you want a cheeseburger?"

"You trying to welch on our deal?"

"No, but wouldn't pizza or tacos be more flavorful?"

"Nope, I've got my taster set."

"Fine, just so you know you have a choice."

She eyeballed me again. I wondered if she could sense the itching I had at the back of my mind. The itching continued through the whole drive, even at the drive-through window. All the way to the campus she said she lived at, I was trying desperately to remember something Vierna had said about visions, and to remember all the details from the one I'd had. It was something about not being able to change the future but that the future wasn't set in stone. Then there was something about the purpose of visions was just to give people time to deal with what was coming before it came.

"When we get to school, I'll take you to find Danny," Therin was saying. "It's just about time for classes to be out for the afternoon, and he doesn't have any night classes this semester."

TWENTY-ONE

We got to the campus just as the sun was setting. Therin was telling me how they both had dorm rooms, even though their parents' house was in Sapulpa, because it made them sad to stay there with their parents gone. Most of the parking lots were empty except for the dorm lots and the lot in front of the concert hall. The wind had calmed, and an early frost was settling in on the grass. It really had been cold after all. Therin directed me to pull around to the third dorm building on the north side of the campus.

"If Danny's here," she said, "He'll probably be in his shorts. I'll go up ahead and let him know you're coming."

I got out when she did and leaned against the nose of the Jeep. It was cold, but the clouds looked to be breaking. Stars twinkled through them here and there, and the grass seemed to return their sparkle. I felt silly for getting all creeped out earlier. It didn't take long for the cold to get uncomfortable, and I hoped Therin would be down soon so I could go up and meet her brother where it was warm enough to be in shorts.

I'd barely thought those thoughts, when she came running down the stairs, tears glittering on her face. At the speed she was coming down, there wasn't going to be a soft stop in her future so I moved to intercept. No sense protecting her from Hurt if she broke her neck now. She nearly bowled me over coming off the stairs and I caught her, holding her steady until she got her balance. She handed me a wrinkled up piece of paper. I read it.

"Dear Therin,

I am so sorry you have to find out like this, but by the time you read this, I might well be dead. I have put you in grave danger and myself as well, I'm afraid. The men who are after me are not what they seem. I am not undercover for the police, I am working for the government. I have been all along. When you read this, I want you to get out. Get out of town immediately. Go to the place where the gardenias bloom in winter. I will meet you there if I survive. I am so sorry for lying to you.

I love you,

Dan"

The paper had been wet and had dried again, and was lightly frosted so it had been there for a while. I had to wonder if he was still alive or not, but the first order of business was to get Therin out of here. I looked up at her, just as fresh tears slid around the bottom of her jaw.

"Where is this place he mentions?"

"It's our parents' house in Sapulpa. We have a sunroom. Maybe he's there already waiting for me."

"Maybe, but we need to get you out of here."

When we turned to go back to the Jeep, the hood was up. I blinked. I blinked again. I had just left it. I looked around the lot, but didn't see anyone near. *How the fuck did they get to it?* I stalked over to see what had been done to it, and as I figured, several of the plug wires were just gone.

"Where is this house in Sapulpa?"

"I can pull it up on your phone as we go."

"Good," I said, handing her my phone. "You do that, I'm going to go requisition us a vehicle."

I grabbed my duffel out of the jeep and Therin grabbed the take-out bag and stuffed it under her arm. I started out across the wide grassy divider between our lot and the one in back of the concert hall, scanning the cars for a potential ride. Therin kept up with me, plugging the information into my phone as we made our way quickly across to the other lot.

We were close to the back lot, and I'd just spotted a promising-looking minivan when there was a flash of greenish light. I looked around to see that Therin had stopped walking. I was still trying to figure out what was wrong with her face when a thin line of blood made its way down the side of her nose from the tiny new hole in her forehead.

I'd never even heard a shot. Baffled, I reached out to hold her. One hand went up to cradle the back of her head as I grappled with her slumping form to try to keep her from hitting the ground. The back of her head was just—gone. I couldn't help it. I sank to the frosted grass with her.

"Aw kiddo," I croaked, my throat and my chest tightening around me. I cried. Just for a minute, and then I got mad. I lifted the phone out of her hand and clasped her hand to my hot cheek. She was already so cold. I stuck the phone in my pocket and pulled my .45.

Slapping the water out of my eyes, I scanned the rooftops. I just caught the silhouette of the shooter ducking back away from the edge of the concert hall roof. I'd led her right into the line of fire. I got up and ran full tilt toward the music hall. If there were men on the ground, this would get their attention. The very same minivan I'd been looking at started up and sped over to the back door of the music hall. Hurt was behind the wheel. The back door flew open and my sniper made for the van. Hurt paused just long enough for the guy to jump in.

Like hell this guy's getting past me again! I kept running at him, only pausing long enough to fire at the van. Two rounds at a time. The van careened towards me. Maybe Hurt figured he'd just run me down, but ultimately it didn't matter. I hopped up on the hood of the next car and pulled the trigger twice more. I put one in Hurt's head and one in the sniper's. The van swerved and smashed into several cars before coming to rest against a light post.

All of the rage that had been keeping me going bled off like I had a bad valve-stem. I had to go and find Therin's brother. Dan might still be in danger if Arlan's hypothesis was right. *Because I have such a stellar track record for keeping people alive...*

I got down off the car and holstered my gun. There would only be three rounds left in the clip. I made my way around the concert hall to the front entrance. I could hear the music when the doors opened. I leaned against the wall for a minute to catch my breath. My chest was on fire again. I guessed it was a wonder I was still alive.

I stood away from the wall and turned around, and was just opening the door, when I realized the music had stopped. Another sound filled the hall. Screaming. Lots of screaming. And crashing followed the screaming. It was coming toward me entirely too fast. Baffled again,

I was still standing there, holding the door open when the inner doors burst open, and people came pouring out. One of them looked like the woman from my vision, and was being pulled along ahead of the chaos by a man I didn't know. They flew past me and I still stood, stunned, at the door. Part of me wanted to believe it was just the smoke Arlan had given me playing up in my system.

Some of the people didn't really look like people anymore. The roiling mass of bloodied and twisted bodies surged forth like a pyroclastic flow. I was still too stunned to move as the first of them fled past me. The first few looked normal enough, but fled in terror from those coming behind. The ones behind them were the fleeing and falling injured, and as some of them fell, the creatures behind them became visible.

People—but not people—with animal or plant features, twisted and grotesque forms that never should have existed took the places of those they felled, and were chased in turn by even more hideous monsters. There were explosions in the distance, but those hardly seemed like a threat compared to the spectacle before me.

Pain ripped through my chest just as the mass of bodies reached me. My entire body seemed to be trying to turn in on itself, and I fell. Conscious thought shattered into a million pieces.

The next thing I knew I was on the concrete and the rush was over. I couldn't stand, but I managed to pull myself into a sitting position. The dead and dying littered the front walk all around me. More and more distant explosions sent tremors through the ground.

There were still screams, but they were fewer and more distant now. I was still trying to process what I'd just seen when one voice cut through the chaos in my head. One rang out above the others, clear and defiant. Her voice. The woman was still alive.

I tried to get up, but my legs were telling me to fuck off. I pulled forward and sat up more, then leaned forward until I was on all fours. Slowly I managed to get them moving enough to crawl. She screamed again. *Goddammit. Move!* Finally I was able to walk my hands up the side of the building and stand, after a fashion. I was on my feet. The pain in my chest was still making it hard to breathe, but I managed to shuffle in the direction of the screams. Soon I was able to walk, and then even half-assed run. Another peal of her voice from the direction of the nature trail. I followed it to a clearing in the woods.

In the clearing was a scene from my vision. The woman was at the bottom of the amphitheater and the creature, who was in the same clothes as the terrified man she'd fled with, had her pinned to the concrete, just as before. She beat at him, kicked and clawed. She fought ferociously. It only seemed to make him more determined,

He held her down and seemed to be sniffing her. First her neck, then her belly, and then her crotch. I pulled my .45 and aimed. He seemed to move a little lower to her thigh and then he bit her. When he sat up with what looked like a chunk of her thigh between his teeth, she went limp, but I had the shot. I fired. The creature fell back, but the woman lay beneath him, unconscious.

I made my way down to her cautiously and rolled the stinking creature off of her. She was still alive. I pulled off my tee shirt and tied it around her thigh as tight as possible. I had to find a safe place to stash her until I was strong enough to get help. I picked her up and started up the stone steps. It took everything I had to get her up to ground level.

Each step after that threatened to be the one that put me—both of us—down. I was pretty sure the numbing of the pain in my chest meant I was dying, but at least it allowed me to carry her, like an overgrown child, back out into the parking lot. I shifted her weight a bit to make it more manageable, and she put her arms around my neck. Her lips brushed lightly against the skin there, and I knew what she was feeling. No. I *felt* what she was feeling. *Safe. Loved.*

I hadn't felt either of those things in a very long time. Then I felt other things too. Things that didn't belong to me. I felt death. I realized suddenly that I was carrying her through a sea of the dead. They were scattered everywhere, but in the doorways of the buildings they were stacked like cordwood. Getting her into a building was not an option.

Something ran past us, snarling and leaving a trail of blood. It didn't notice us, and I didn't attract its attention. It seemed to be a sort of insect, but it was man-sized, not to mention twisted and bleeding. Two large flying things chased after it. There was a sort of squealing that broke off in a squelching sound as the flying things caught up with their quarry. I didn't look back. I carried her out to the street that ran in front of the college and turned back toward downtown and the hospital. *Toni—are you alive? Please be alive.*

As I stumbled down the street, the scenery only grew more and more dismal. Although the bodies seemed to thin out a bit, there were cars abandoned or wrecked along the street, their occupants who knew where. There were so many fires burning you couldn't see more than a block or two for the smoke. I passed by what I thought was a tree, only to have it snap at me with what looked like pincers at the ends of its branches.

Pausing for a moment to rest under a bridge, I got hissed at by something that might once have been a cat, but now bore a striking resemblance to a hairy scorpion. I decided to press on. Closer to downtown, I saw what I thought at first must be looters, darting into shops with the windows broken out, only to realize that what they were carrying out wasn't merchandise. It was people. One pair I thought was making out in an alley was actually one black-eyed, bloated looking female who was enjoying a dinner of warm deli clerk. She gurgle-growled at me, and I kept walking. I couldn't have compared her to anything more closely than to a tick.

I had to get this girl off the street, but there was nowhere safe anymore. Just then the whine and roar of a motorcycle making good time coming up from behind caught my attention and I turned, hoping to get the person's attention. Its headlight dodged deftly back and forth between the abandoned cars. The bike slowed as it approached us.

Kane Quinn stopped the bike a few feet back and levelled a sawed-off at my head. He flicked on a flashlight attached to the gun.

"Step forward and show me your eyes," he ordered. I did as he said, and made sure he could see the woman.

"Still human?"

"Yeah, still human, I think."

"Got another one huh? Where you going with this one?"

"Hospital downtown or the hotel down south of it. Either one is fine. Where the hell have you been?"

"Tracking Hurt, like you. I was on my way to the college, but I had to stop and ride the shit-storm out. I guess he's in the middle of all this. And there is no south of the hospital. If there was a hotel there, it's history. A couple of plane crashes and the fires from them took out the whole south side."

"Hospital then. Hurt's dead." My heart sank, but I still hoped somehow they'd vacated in time.

"Here then," Quinn said getting off of the bike. "You take it, I'll get another one. Get her out of here."

"Quinn. Thanks."

"Yeah," he said holding her up while I got on. He hefted her onto the back of the bike, and she just adapted, laying her head naturally on my shoulder and sliding her arms around my waist. Kane cocked an eyebrow, and said, "Keep that one. Now git."

I gave him a nod, and then turned the bike toward downtown and the hospital. No way was I letting this one get away.

TWENTY-TWO

I tried to steer clear of the worst parts, but downtown was a warzone. I worried that if she woke she would freak out, so I opted for speed and efficiency over caution at the end. I only made the mistake of stopping at a stoplight once. The thing that rushed us looked even stranger than the creatures I'd seen so far. I couldn't even begin to describe it, I just drew and shot it. That was when I'd realized my count had been off. I should have been out.

I didn't stop again. There was so much blood that the street was slick with it, and it slowed our progress, but we were almost there. My guts did a sudden flip. *Is this everywhere? Is this the spell? If Therin was the last sacrifice, then my failure did this.*

I carefully turned the corner into the hospital entrance and did the last few yards at a snail's pace, weaving between the bodies. *Bungling Agent destroys the world, news at ten.*

The parking lot was stacked with bodies, so I pulled right up to the ER doors. I dropped the kickstand and climbed off carefully, holding the woman up as I did. Then I lifted her off the bike, and cradled her again as I made for the sliding door. It didn't open. There were still assorted screams and crying from all around. It was bedlam out here. I walked over to the little door and maneuvered it open enough to catch it with my foot. Then I got a leg in and opened it wider and squeezed us through. The main lights were out, and it looked like they were running on emergency power. There was moaning and some soft crying in the lobby, but it was quieter here. Calmer.

An empty gurney sat against one wall in the hallway, and I laid her there. I looked up and down the hall in triage, and there were no doctors, nurses or orderlies to be seen. There was a staff room at the end of the hall. I headed that way, pushing the gurney along with me. I didn't want to leave her alone. I was a little worried about what I might find, so I drew the .45. Then I remembered the ammunition situation and laid it on the gurney beside her. There was a light on in the little room, and a figure sat hunched up in one corner, rocking. I opened the door quietly and poked my head in.

It hit me hard. Fear, sorrow, anguish, pain. Wave after wave of it. Her fear, her sorrow, her pain. I felt it, but it didn't come from me. It was coming from her. I shivered. I was afraid to try working on the woman I'd brought in by myself, but this nurse was clearly in no shape. She was not handling any of this, not that I could blame her. The poor thing wasn't just rocking either, she was banging her head softly against the cabinet door. Worry was what hit me next. She must have family out there somewhere and she couldn't get to them.

"Hello?" I called in softly, hoping not to startle her. Nothing in her emotions changed. She didn't even realize I was there. I walked in slowly, sensing her emotions, letting them wash over me. *Shit. I'm one of them now. Like Therin.*

I laid a hand on her shoulder. The feelings only got more intense. I wanted to scream, to cry, to hide. Anything to make it stop hurting so bad and to stop being afraid. And then again, as soon as I'd made that connection, another feeling welled up from her. There was a fluttering of something akin to happiness—hope?

She turned to look into my eyes. The flutter vanished. It was like somebody stomped on a butterfly. In its place came nothing. There was just a hole. I knew then that she had been hoping for a loved one to be crouching there beside her, waiting to lift her out of that hell. There was only me. I must have looked like every other damned deranged person left here.

"I know," I said, smoothing the rumpled shoulder of her uniform, "I know you were hoping for someone else. Family maybe. But what if they're on their way here, or what if they're here somewhere and need your help?"

She looked at me again, and a little of that flutter returned. What she needed right now, what she really needed—even from her family—was to be needed. I wondered briefly if I looked like one of those monsters.

"You have to be strong," I said, "There's nothing you can do in here, but there's plenty you can do out there." My own pain returned with a vengeance and I winced, unable to stop it in time. I ran a hand over my scarred chest to appease the pain somewhat. "People are dying and we need you. You can save us. I have one person right here by the door if you can't go outside right now."

She teared up, but she nodded her head. The flutter became a full purr, and she seemed to strengthen as she said, "I'll take a look."

Her recovery made me almost tear up too, but more than that, it made me smile—despite the pain. It felt like the first real smile I'd smiled in thirty years. Like it replaced all the horrors and all the anger. I held a hand out to her and helped her up onto her feet. I offered to roll the gurney in, but the nurse said she'd go out to her. She untied the shirt and lifted it gently off of the woman's wound.

"Oh my," she said, "I'm going to need help with this. She's lost a lot of blood."

"Sure, whatever she needs. My boss, if she's still alive, will make sure the bills get paid."

"Sweetie," she said sweetly, "I don't think there's going to be bills anymore."

She went to the nurses' station and picked up the intercom phone. She clicked the button and her voice came over all the speakers in the hospital.

"Attention all staff remaining, please report to the first floor central nurses station for mandatory briefing. Repeat, all remaining staff to the first floor central nurses' station. If you are injured or trapped, try to reach a call button. We will come and find you. Again, if you are a Doctor, nurse, orderly or other hospital staff, please come to the first floor central nurses' station. Let's get this hospital back in business."

Within minutes there were people crowding around the nurses' station and the nurse from the lounge put a team to work on the woman I'd brought in.

Then she started organizing teams to go through the hospital. As I watched the staff swing into action, the pain in my chest finally won out. I lost my footing and went down. Nobody noticed at first, they were busy with their work. Then, as the team worked furiously to save the woman on the gurney, one of the nurses went down too. She began to convulse on the floor, and I could hear her bones breaking.

One of the assisting nurses opened a surgical pack and removed a scalpel. He reached down deftly and swiftly opened the writhing nurse's throat, then stood back up to finish his work on the woman atop the gurney. No one else missed a beat. The light was fading around me.

The darkness that embraced me was warm and comfortable. There was no more pain. The woman would be saved and my job was done, for better or worse. I could rest now. I'd failed to save the world. The world I knew was dying. I would never see it again. It only seemed right that I should die with it.

I was on the precipice again. This time Therin was beside me. We watched together as the great swell advanced on the little village and overtook it. There was no reason to run this time. There was nothing to be done.

"Where are we?" I asked Therin. She turned to look at me. She was perfect. There was no blood. No hole in her head.

"Right where we were," she said, her green eyes boring into my own. "Nothing has changed, Max. You still have a job to do."

"But everything has changed. And if I'm dead..."

"Do you feel dead? You kind of look dead, but you're not. I am."

"Therin, I'm so sorry."

"Quit it. You didn't do this. You have to stick around and make sure these yo-yo's get through this mess without the whole human race going extinct."

"But what does all this mean? How come I keep seeing this village, and this storm?"

"It's your head, what the hell are you asking me for? You'll figure it out. Now get back there, they need you."

"What can I do when this wave thing is so much bigger than me?"

"See, you're figuring it out already," she said. She smiled mysteriously and vanished.

I woke up in a hospital gown. I was in a bed in a room. The window was open. It was daylight outside, and nearly silent inside. Outside there were assorted shouts and movements, somewhere a bird was singing. I wondered what that bird might look like. There was a bed beside mine, and on it was the woman from the college.

I was hooked up to an old-school gravity IV, and so was she. I checked the bag, and satisfied it was just glucose, I removed the tube from the back of my hand and crimped off the feed. It stung like a sonofabitch, but I felt a hundred percent better. I fished around and found some tape and a cotton ball. I wrapped the hole up tight to stop the bleeding and looked around for my clothes.

All I found were a couple of spare gowns, some of those stupid paper shoes and my phone and wallet. I tied one of the spare gowns on backward to cover my exposed rear, and slipped on the paper shoes.

I sat the phone and wallet on the end of the bed and pulled the clipboards off of the beds to look them over.

Her injuries were pretty deep, but the artery was missed by a fraction of an inch. She was in a coma, but otherwise seemed healthy. Mine said something about some chest x-rays being inconclusive, and blood being absorbed into my skin, but were really hard to read. The envelope with the images was attached, as was another envelope with the images from my last visit to radiology.

I held the pages one by one up to the light from the open window. The old ones showed the needle-like sliver of bone that was causing all of my pain. It was circled in red grease pencil and marked "bone sliver?" I was a little afraid to look at the new set, but I couldn't help myself. The second set showed the same area, circled in red by a different hand with a similar pencil, and absent the bone sliver. Question marks hung outside the circle. Their question all too obvious. *Where the hell did it go?*

I couldn't stay here. The woman was going to be alright, but who knew what they might make of me if I stayed. I tucked all of the x-rays into one of the envelopes along with my wallet and phone and tied it up into the other spare gown, then made for the door. I had to find Toni if she was alive, and Daniel. I had to tell him about Therin. How she died trying to save the world.

Where the hell might he even be in all this mess? The place where the gardenias bloom in winter. The address had been in Sapulpa.

TWENTY-THREE

The ride to Sapulpa wasn't as bad as I had imagined. Once I hit the outskirts of town, the bodies and fires thinned out to where the air was almost breathable. There were still stretches of road that would have been impassible by car, but the motorcycle made it through without too much trouble.

It was on the long stretch of I-244 between the towns that I noticed other things that weren't right. There were patches of trees that seemed to writhe without any wind to move them. Something flew over my head that looked like a snake, but had wings and feathers. I swear it took a snap at me as it flew over.

What looked like a group of men on horseback stood atop a low ridge overlooking the highway as I was just getting into Sapulpa. As I got closer, they started coming down the hill. At a run. Maybe they wanted help, and maybe they wanted to warn me off, but I didn't have time for them either way.

I sped up to get past them, and as they closed in on my right flank, I saw that they weren't men on horseback at all. Maybe they had been before. Now they were centaurs, for all intents and purposes. I gunned it. It was a good thing I did too, because those guys could move. One of them reached a hand out as I passed him and nearly snatched me off the motorcycle.

Pulling into town, I did see people that looked alright for the most part, but they were generally uneasy and dirty. They wandered aimlessly or ducked into buildings as I passed.

There were also changed people. They mostly didn't look like the dog people or the ticks, but they looked like they had been combined with other things.

One man had scales and was beating the hell out of a fire hydrant, looking for all the world like he was having an asthma attack. A woman on the corner by the courthouse was covered in fur, all the way to the top of her little upright triangle ears. *Cat?*

I was kind of handling things until I rounded the corner onto the street the house was supposed to be on. The creature on the sidewalk looked for all the world like a coiled snake, and I would have gone on without a second glance if a stray cat hadn't tried to run past the thing, only to find itself impaled on its wickedly barbed tail.

The thing held up its prey as I came near and then, turning its attention to me, barked as I rolled by. The cat twitched a couple of times, and the snake-dog thing retracted the barbs on its tail spike and the cat slid off, landing lifeless on the sidewalk. That shit was too messed up.

The house was small for a two-story, but its size left plenty of room in the back yard for a large solarium in back. This was much larger than the cozy little sunroom I'd imagined when she'd spoken of it. This was why the gardenias bloomed in winter. I could see them from the street. I watched for a moment before I got off the cycle. I was anxious to get indoors, but I was also a little worried about what might be inside. Especially in the solarium. Finally, I put the kickstand down and walked up to the door. I hadn't even knocked yet when it opened and a large bore gun barrel peered out at me.

"State your business at this house." The man's accent was Scottish. That couldn't be right.

"I'm looking for Daniel Caldwell. I have to speak to him on an urgent matter of family business."

"I know Daniel Caldwell, and you're no kin of his."

"No, I have news is all."

The door swung open and a thin man with spiky brown hair stood behind the shotgun, which followed my every move. He motioned me to move into the house, and I did, making sure to keep my hands visible.

"Have a seat," he said. "I'm Daniel Caldwell. What do you know about my family?"

A volatile mix of emotions poured off the man. Our eyes locked, only for a moment, but that was enough. The nose of the gun dropped to the floor. Daniel's shoulders drooped. He shook his head. There were no words spoken, but I could feel his whole world crashing around him. I couldn't look at him anymore.

"I'm sorry," were the only words I could manage.

Daniel dropped all defense. He stumbled and then sat, his face frozen in horror and pain. Perhaps the worst part was that the poor man couldn't even engage in denial. He'd seen it all, everything that happened in my thoughts. He knew what I knew. He saw—everything that I had seen. There was a long silence. We sat, sharing our grief, speaking none of it.

Suddenly I felt like a fraud. Could my grief even be real? I'd only known her for a few days. This man had known her her whole life. He was her brother. Probably. Why would he have a Scottish accent? Why were his eyes brown when hers were green? Daniel's grief was undeniable, but mine? Was it just guilt? Our strained reverie was broken by the sound of car doors. We both got up to look out the windows.

"Who did you say you worked for?" Daniel was actually surprised.

"The office of Human Protection. I didn't really say, but I figured you'd pick it out, being a Telepath."

"She told you?" His eyes flashed angry for a moment before they remembered their pain. "Well, I guess we'd better let them in."

He opened the door and welcomed in Dr. Pape, Toni, Kai, and the single agent that had accompanied them into his home. I noticed there was no NSA guy, and no assistant accompanying Dr. Pape. Toni was disheveled, but whole, as was Dr. Pape. Kai looked like he'd been ill, but was physically unchanged. The agent that kept him in custody seemed untouchable. And his hair was perfect.

Daniel, it seemed, had noticed. And he thought the guy was handsome. That knowledge made me immediately uncomfortable in the extreme. It didn't feel right to know things like that without being told. People's emotions on that level were private, and I felt like an intruder, but I didn't know how to stop it.

I looked at Toni to try and take my mind off Daniel and his emotions, only to bump into hers as she caught my gaze. She wanted me. She was deeply afraid on a lot of levels at the same time. She was worried about me and somehow resentful of worrying about me as well.

I shook my head.

"Max, are you alright?" It was Dr. Pape speaking, but I couldn't look at her. I dropped my gaze to the floor. I couldn't look at anybody. I didn't want to know what they were feeling. I had to get out of here. I strode to the door, and went out without a word, letting it slam lazily behind me.

Outside, the crisp air help ease the overheated feeling I'd had. It wasn't long before Daniel was standing beside me. Just who I didn't want to see.

"I know what you're thinking."

"Yeah," I said with more bite than I'd intended, "because you're a telepath."

"No, it's not like that. Well sometimes it is. What I mean is that I know what you're going through right now."

"Yeah. Well, maybe you can tell me how to make it stop then. I just felt stuff I was never supposed to feel."

"You can't. Empathy sucks, like telepathy, because it doesn't have a switch. You have to learn how to focus. Look, I'm no expert, but if you ever need to talk or someone to practice with, I'm here." The emotion coming from him now was hopeful. Still sad, but reaching out.

"Thanks," I said, "And I'm not gay, by the way."

"Yeah, I got that too," he said chuckling.

"Hm. Hey, where's Arlan and that other guy?"

"Dr. Pape said Arlan went back north, and the NSA liaison—changed. Donald had to kill him or he would have eaten them all."

"Your kung fu is the best."

"I know right?"

We went back in to join the others. I asked Dr. Pape about Arlan and the others, and I made sure to ask about that Chamberlain guy.

"Oh, he went with Arlan."

"You let them go to DC alone?"

"We didn't really have a choice. Someone had to go back and find out the state of the government. We have to know if continuity was preserved or if we're just going to have to create a new one."

"Oh," I said, clamming up. I did feel better knowing someone else got it, and would have my back, but not enough to get all chatty.

"We need to establish a base of operations and communications," she continued. "Much of the infrastructure has been destroyed, so we'll need to work with HAM and shortwave, to replace telephones. We'll need radios and receivers, and a location. Preferably somewhere on a hill."

"I think I know just the spot," I chimed in, "It's just on the edge of town, and sits on a hill between two highways and next to a railroad. I can show you."

"Good," she said, and then led the way out the door. Daniel offered to drive Dr. Pape in the Lincoln, and Toni opted to ride with me. I couldn't have refused if I'd wanted to. Which I didn't.

For once her emotions were so clear to me that I thought I might actually understand her. I led them up Highway 97 hill to the steel shop. It was abandoned as I had figured.

"Oh," Toni said as we pulled into the wreckage of the steel shop's parking lot. 'That meteor. Wow, Max, how do you get so lucky?"

"Maybe I'm born with it," I said, eliciting a giggle from her. It wasn't a flirt, exactly.

"I'm sorry," she said.

The others exited the Lincoln and surveyed the scene. There were antennas already on the roof that we might be able to use. There might even be a HAM in there somewhere. The walk-in door was secured with a padlock and hasp. It was a wonder no one had broken it yet.

Daniel stepped up beside me, holding something shiny out in his palm. I feigned surprise and gestured for him to do the honors.

He opened the lock and we filed into the dark, shelving-lined front bay. The office was small and took up only a ten by ten area of the shop's large, sprawling footprint. Behind it was a wire mesh wall that seemed to block off a hallway and another set of small rooms. Using flashlights and phone lights, we moved back to the little office and scanned it for equipment. There was a CB and a police scanner, but there was no HAM radio.

"Say we found this stuff," I said, "how are we going to power it with the grid down?"

"Once we get our people all together we'll start on it." Dr. Pape lit up as many dark corners as possible with her little pen-light. "This will do for now, but it's too visible to work for long. Judging by those dents in the siding, this building can take a punch."

"Meteor strike," I said helpfully, "right outside."

A scuffling sound behind me brought my attention back to Kai. He was being sat in a folding chair by the guy Daniel had called Donald. Donald ordered him to sit right there, but knowing Kai, I knew that wasn't going to be enough of an incentive. Glancing over the contents of the desk, I didn't see anything immediately useful for tying him up. I ducked in behind the desk and searched the shelves underneath, coming up with just what I needed.

I strode toward Kai—maybe looking like I wanted to kill him, maybe not—and Donald reached out an arm to stop me. I knocked it out of my way. I was going to get some answers from this little traitor. Donald grabbed my shoulder and I spun around and punched him, sending him sprawling. Then I leaned over and snatched the knife from Donald's belt.

Kai was working himself up to a standing position to try and run, but I got to him first, putting him back in the chair, hard. I leaned forward, putting my hands on top of his shoulders. I smiled my most menacing smile.

"I have a knife and some duct tape," I growled in his face, "Can you guess what I'm thinking?"

Fear rolled off him like a gray-green body odor. *So it turns out people really can reek of fear—good.* Only it didn't really feel good. It wasn't so much a real smell as it was an impression of one—a resonance with those things in his mind. It disgusted me. There was something else there too, hidden— but not well. Daniel and Donald had ahold of my shoulders by then, and were dragging me back away from Kai. I let them. I'd made my point, mostly. I did offer a parting gift, though.

"There will be answers, weasel." I said through gritted teeth. "You little son-of-a-bitch. Your Pele can't protect you from me. Not anymore." Kai knew about Mama Vierna and her voodoo practice. He knew what I was capable of physically. What he didn't know was that I'd changed inside. Nothing more needed to be said for now. I turned and stalked toward the outside door.

"Hurt was the low man on the totem pole!" Kai called after me. Toni and Dr. Pape leaned out of the little office door to listen, either drawn by the scuffle or by his sudden cry. "I don't know how high it went or who all is involved, but Hurt got his orders from someone else."

"Tell us something we don't know." I said, stopping mid-stride and not turning to look at him, "Why should we believe a damn word that crawls its way out of your infernal pie hole?"

"Because I can get back in."

I don't know if it was what he said, or the fact that he had the balls to say anything at all, but I turned back around. Nobody moved.

I stalked back over to him and this time nobody stopped me as I put my hands back on his shoulders and brought them in to almost close around his scrawny neck. I wanted him dead.

The rage wasn't just for his betrayal. It was for Therin. For Claire and Jack and who knew how many dead and dying. For all of the ones who might actually live through this abomination and live with whatever they'd become. Friend or not, offer of help or not, he was guilty of the highest possible treason and of genocide. He deserved to die.

I had my jaw clenched so hard it hurt. I looked up from my prey. Toni stood behind him now, but how she'd gotten there I didn't know. Her eyes were enormous and pleading. Fear flowed from all around me to meld with the sadness coming from her.

My hands still around Kai's neck, I looked over to Dr. Pape. Her face was stone, but she was afraid as well. *Is she afraid for Kai or of me?* Either way, it was enough to quell the rage for now. I let Kai go and walked out. I had to find a place to think. I took the Lincoln. If they could get it through, so could I.

TWENTY-FOUR

The front door of the Gold Rush Lounge was off its hinges. I crept up to the little strip-mall bar slowly, adjusting the now-mostly-empty duffel across my back, listening, and hearing nothing. I peeked around the doorjamb and saw no one moving around inside. It reeked of nicotine and stale beer, mingled with the rusty tang of blood. Part of me felt like the world's biggest heel, stepping over bodies for booze, and another said I'd have to get used to stepping over them. We were going to need supplies. The fact that I was looking to get shitfaced directly had no bearing on the subject.

Once I was sure it was clear, I walked in and checked the storeroom behind the bar, just to be positive. There was no one. I set the bag on the bar and loaded it with all the bottles I thought I could carry.

Most of it I had no intention of drinking, but the Patron was mine. And the rum. And maybe the bourbon. Once the bag was full, I zipped it and went back to the storeroom to see what they had in cases. I picked up a case of longnecks and figured if all went well after I got this and the bag loaded into the Lincoln, I'd come back for the rest.

I lugged the case to the bar and set it down long enough to slowly lift the duffel and rest the handles on my shoulder. Then I grabbed the case and lugged all out the door. I put the duffel in the passenger seat and the case in the back. I closed the doors and cast a glance up the highway.

That herd of centaurs I'd spotted before—at least I figured it was them— perked their heads up. I hadn't seen them when I went in. There was a moment's hesitation as the leader and I watched each other intently. Then he snorted. A chorus of whoops and yells rose up as the entire herd burst into motion. They were fast.

I scrambled around the car and got in, but starting it proved a little tricky since my hands were shaking. I got it going and slammed it into reverse just as one of them reached for the car. He managed to grab hold of the rearview mirror on my side, and it snapped, but he lost his hold on it and the broken mirror clunked dully against the door as I wheeled the car around and shifted into drive. I was just in the process of flooring it when I heard a series of thumps and sharp cracks that I also felt through the floorboard.

I'd been so intent of watching the centaurs that I hadn't seen the board that was now splintering under the weight of the car.

There was a flat. Maybe two. Somewhere in the back of my mind was the notion that the board hadn't been there before either. Something was smoking from underneath the Lincoln. There was no time for the tire and lube spiel, so I floored it. The car screamed out of the parking lot, streaming smoke and the rubber flapping. About a block from the turnoff to 166, the check engine light came on. The centaurs were bearing down on me, coming fast. The car was slowing.

It was probably a good thing, as I would have flipped it in the turn otherwise. As it was, first one tire and then the other peeled off the rims as the car rounded the corner. I gunned it as hard as I could, but there were still the next corner, the railroad tracks and the hill to climb.

The car screeched around the second turn, and hit hard at the tracks, but came out the other side still screaming. The bare rims threw sparks off the old faded pavement of 166 and she started up the hill moving fairly well for a dying machine.

I'd lost sight of the centaurs going around the curves, but I doubted that the corners would be enough to keep them off my trail. The car was still slowing, but I found a spot about halfway up the hill to turn up an old gravel driveway. It was still going up, it just veered off of the main road. The car was smoking to beat hell, rattling and beginning to sputter. About a hundred yards in, the engine gave up and the car died completely.

I could just make out a barn roof further up the driveway. This being the hill behind the plant, I hoped that I could get there without too much trouble, but if I led those centaurs back... well, I couldn't lead them back to the others. I unzipped the bag, snagged a bottle of Patron, stuffed it in the floorboard and lit out for the barn, bottle in hand. Oddest thing was, as I sprinted up the partly wooded hill, I felt more alive than I had in weeks.

Glass broke behind me. They'd already found the car, and were unleashing their fury on it. *How much of their human intelligence do they still have? Enough to set a trap for me at the bar?* Not taking the time to look back, I threw open the barn door, which hung heavy with chains that clanked as I opened it. If I had time, I could chain the doors, but the hoof-beats and hollering outside told me they'd already tracked me to the barn.

I tucked the bottle into the waistband of my pants and climbed up the ladder to the loft. I was almost at the top when the door flew open again and some of the centaurs thudded into the barn. They huffed and stomped, but soon went back out the way they came. None of them had even looked up.

I sneaked over to the loft window and peered out through the cracks. They were still down there, milling around and huffling. I heard no words spoken, but all at once they all turned the same direction and thundered off back the way they'd come. I figured this was as good a place as any to sit and think, so I swung open the loft window and sat back against a half-rotted hay bale with my thoughts and my hard-won bottle of Patron, and proceeded to get to the bottom of it.

I woke to the sound of Toni's voice calling my name. It was biting cold, I had a raging hangover, and something sharp was poking me in the neck. And the armpit. I was still in the barn, and her voice was carrying over from the steel shop a few hundred yards away to the west. The sun should have been shining, but it was dimmed by a hideous layer of smoke and who knew what else. The whole sky was a sick gray-yellow.

I climbed down. I had to shut her up before the centaurs or something worse heard her and made a meal out of her. Plus I figured I'd have to face the music for yesterday. I had a hard time pinpointing the direction of her voice, so I started back down toward the car, thinking to triangulate from down there and get a better fix on her location.

I checked over my shoulder frequently for stray centaurs, but the only thing I saw was a tree at the end of the driveway that seemed to be singing. When I got close to it, I saw that it didn't have bark, it had flesh. Not only did it have silvery flesh, it had a face. A delicate, feminine face, haloed by the most slender, willow-like purple leaves. The effect was enchanting.

She cooed to me as I passed, I felt only longing and serenity from her, but was too wary to approach. Something about it reminded me of Ulysses. Finally, I stepped just a foot or so closer. She was rooted to the spot, so all I really had to do was stay just out of reach. I reached out a hand, and she reached out a branch. It was warm, and leathery to the touch, as if she were just a girl wearing soft gloves.

Swiftly, much of my discomfort slid off like snakeskin. Now that I was close, I could make out a vaguely human shape to the trunk. I broke the connection with a pang of regret. I couldn't believe how serene she was in the midst of all that was happening—had happened— to her. I stepped back onto the road and looked back. She was just beautiful.

I left her with a nod, and started back up the hill, and though my head still hurt, it was better, and the rest of me felt just about ship-shape. I covered the remaining ground pretty quick. Toni was standing on the side parking lot when I reached it. She ran out to me and I held my arms out. She slapped the piss out of me, ringing my ears and bringing my headache back with a vengeance. I was just glad she hadn't punched me.

"What was the point of taking off like that?"

"Good morning to you too," I said, rubbing my jaw, "Rough night?"

"I don't suppose you've got breakfast in that bag?"

"Sure, if you don't mind Jimmy Walker or Jim Beam hanging out for breakfast."

"You're an idiot."

"It's been a rough couple of days, I thought maybe we could use a little relaxation."

"What we could use is food, water and working hands."

My ears were burning. Feeling her disappointment was what really stung. She looked angry, but what she really felt was hurt. I'd been an asshole again.

When I should have stepped up, I fell down. When I should have been on watch, I abandoned my post. Maybe I was just that kind of jackass.

She stormed off and I didn't blame her. There wasn't a hole in the world deep enough to hide my shame anymore. I followed her back, setting the bag down just inside the door. I cast a long look at Kai as I passed him, just to remind him of where we stood. I was just thinking about slinking back out the door when Daniel took hold of my arm.

"Come on then," he said, You want to go get stuff, you can come with me, we're going shopping."

I didn't say anything, and he didn't explain, but I felt a mix of confidence and frustration coming from him.

He led me to a moving van parked in the front lot just as a trio of backhoes rumbled in and began dumping loads of dirt into the crater that occupied much of the lot. The noise did nothing to help the headache. I got in the van and closed to door to lessen the noise. Daniel got into the driver's side.

"What are we shopping for?"

"Food, supplies, and people."

"Huh?" It was all I could manage.

"We need stuff. We need people to help put some organization back in this organization. Things don't get done without people to do them. We're going down into Sapulpa to see if there's anyone still alive who's interested."

"I really don't think—shouldn't you take Donald instead?"

"Nope," he said, blushing so that his whole head turned red. "He's keeping watch. You're the one for this job."

"There's centaurs on 66," I said. "I think they're patrolling."

"Yeah, we saw them when we drove into town yesterday." He didn't say anything else, but I knew he'd picked up on my guilt, and the fact that he didn't rub it in spoke volumes about the man. Once upon a time I wouldn't have cared what someone else thought of me. Things had changed.

We went down 97 hill into Sapulpa, passing the newly burned out Mexican restaurant and the now-derelict gas station. I wondered if there would still be gas in the tanks.

Daniel managed getting the truck around the abandoned vehicles okay, but it got me thinking that we might be able to clear a path if we had the right equipment and manpower. It wasn't likely anyone else was going to. Still, the streets in Sapulpa were a lot clearer than those in Tulsa. Most people in this sleepy town had likely been home already when the wave hit.

It was a wave. Not a wave of water like the vision, but one of change.

Every time we spotted someone, we stopped and asked if they needed help and if they'd want to help us in return to get things back up and running. Most people just wanted to be left to their grief. Still, by the time we were about two-thirds of the way through town there were maybe a dozen people in the back of the truck.

We pulled in at the big chain drugstore on the corner, and could see from across the street that the main grocery store had already been looted. There was a Greasey's Burger catty-corner to us that looked intact and Daniel pulled in there. He put the truck in park and we scanned for signs of life. There weren't any. I opened my door to get out, and Daniel put a hand on my shoulder.

He handed me the Mossberg from the dash and held out six extra shells. He grabbed the pistol from the console and opened the back to get the others to follow us in and carry stuff. Then we went to see if they were serving lunch. The one person inside was deceased. Probably the waitress that was closing the night before. She was hard to look at. Not because she was dead, but because she was *wrong*.

Her body was twisted and her skin had become green and coarse, sandpapery. There were leaves that had sprouted from her in places and withered after she died. The crown of her head had opened up into sections and a beige, cotton-like substance fluffed up through the opening. It was the same with her hands. A memory from growing up near the cotton fields halted all further reason on the subject of what had become of her. *Not cotton-like. She turned into cotton. She combined with her cotton uniform, and didn't survive the spell.*

"Grab whatever you can," Daniel spoke into the metallic silence, startling me, "Food, drinks, whatever. Anything useful." The others filed in and started to go through the place. I headed back and opened up the walk-in, propping it open with a bag of sugar.

As I did, a couple of the women we'd picked up filed in and started gathering things up, but as the first woman came to the door, I reached for the load she was carrying.

Turning, I found a guy behind me, so I handed it to him and turned around for another load. Our spontaneous work line had the walk-in emptied in minutes, and another one had formed to clear the pantry.

We were just loading the last of the Styrofoam cups and plates into the truck, when a sickeningly familiar "pop" made everything stop. Daniel went down. I couldn't catch him because I was looking for the shooter. I found him too, nestled between the rails on the other side of the little bridge just down Main Street from the driveway entrance. The guy was quick, but I was pissed.

I took half the width of the narrow two-lane bridge in two broad running steps, and then leapt, managing to hook an arm around the little bastard's throat. My lunge had taken us over the side of the bridge, and we tumbled together down the muddy creek bank, taking our licks from the rocks and scrub brush as we went.

I got him by the back of his shirt collar and stood. The creek water only came up to my waist. He flailed and lurched. He swung and kicked. I only twisted harder. All the rage I had put down before came flooding back and I wanted nothing more than to squeeze and twist.

I could feel his surprise. His panic. As he grew weaker for lack of oxygen, I felt a momentary sadness from him. And then I felt nothing. The nothing felt good.

I let the man's body fall forward and left him face down in the creek. I was done with letting the bastards kill people I cared about. As I climbed back up the creek bank I wondered if he was one of those Shadow Council people. It didn't matter. I was going to put down anyone who came at me or mine. And I was going to find this Shadow Council and rip it apart. With my bare hands. I trudged back to the truck to find Daniel already bandaged and being tended. Apparently some of these folks had skills.

"You're alive," I said, only mildly surprised.

"And the other guy?"

"I got him," I said. Shaking my head, "He won't get a second shot."

I held out a hand and Daniel shook it. I shook his hand away and stuck mine out again. I made sure to clear my thoughts. It was high time I messed with him a little. *Confusion, hurt and something else—embarrassment?* Suddenly I couldn't help grinning.

"Gimme the keys, Doofidgit"

"Really," Daniel said, "I take a bullet in the line of duty and that's what you've got for me? Doofidgit?"

"Only until I can think of something more demeaning." He handed over the keys and I helped him to the passenger door, got him in and drove the whole kit and caboodle up the hill.

When we reached the steel shop, Donald came out to meet us. I got out and rolled up the cargo door to let people out. Donald went around to the passenger side, and seeing the bandage on Daniel's head, opened the door to help him out.

There was a flutter of feeling from Donald. It was like the hope I had felt back at the hospital, but lighter. It was similar to the impulse of attraction I'd felt from Daniel earlier, but less sure. As soon as Daniel was on the ground, Donald embraced him and gave him a kiss that removed any doubt about how they felt.

It was like in the cartoons when the character turns all red and steam shoots out from around its neck. That was the level of discomfort. I was intruding, but I couldn't help it. This was me now. This was something I would have to learn to handle. Somehow.

Maybe if I used it to suss out Kai's intentions, it wouldn't get me in trouble elsewhere. I wasn't used to all this feeling shit, and it was weighing heavy on me. I walked into the building and saw that Kai was no longer seated in the middle of the main room. I went to the little office and knocked. Then I peeked in.

Toni was alone in the little room. Scribbling furiously, she glanced up and waved for me to come in with one hand while continuing to write with the other. Finally she gave me her full attention. She stood and came around to the front of the desk to lean on it, facing me. For the first time I noticed her legs were covered in bruises. I couldn't notice that right now.

"He in here?"

"If you mean Kai," Toni said, "the answer is no. You two don't need to be breathing the same air anyway. He can't get dead before he stands trial or tells us what he knows or both."

"I'm not going to kill him."

"You sure looked like it yesterday."

"I looked like a lot of things yesterday that I'll deny for the rest of my life. I need to see him. He'll talk to me, and I can tell when he's lying now. Besides I already killed a guy today, so my till is topped up."

"Well, I kinda wrung—"

"No, wait," she said. "Go back to where you said you could tell when he's lying now."

"Oh. I can do that now. I kind of feel other people's feelings. I'm an empath or some shit."

"An-empath-or-some-shit—" She looked a lot like she was going to smack me again.

"I was going to tell you—I..." I stopped when her shoulders slumped.

"How long?"

"Since the wave hit. It hit me, and there was a sliver left in my chest and Therin's blood and..." She stiffened, her arms coming up to cross her chest. She stood away from the desk now, closing the space between us slightly and widening her stance defiantly.

"And you're just now telling me?"

"Yeah."

"And how am I feeling now, Max?"

As I looked at her the full impact of my words hit me like lightning. I had no excuse, and now I couldn't speak. The name of the feeling was betrayal, and I couldn't say it.

"C'mon Max, it doesn't take an empath!" She waited, but I was paralyzed. "You're hopeless." She moved to pass by me and accidentally brushed against my shoulder. I clamped down on the desperation I felt then, I wanted so badly to stop her. To hold her. She stopped before she got to the door.

"Toni—" I turned.

"Oh, my god," she said, turning back to face me again. This time her eyes were wide and full of water. "It all makes sense now! Max. Ah, God. Max, I'm so sorry."

"Please," I gulped, "Don't be. Empathy sucks, but I think pity is the worst."

When she reached up to cradle my face in her hands and planted a small soft kiss on my chin, it wasn't pity that I felt from her. There was no disappointment, no resentment, there was only a flutter like the yellowy joy of a springtime sun. Then just as swiftly, something overshadowed that sun. No wonder I'd never understood women. I wondered how they ever understood themselves.

TWENTY-FIVE

"You felt it when she died? Daniel's sister? Were you two—close?"

"No. And no. She was a good kid, but we weren't romantic. And I didn't have this thing until after. I think she was the final sacrifice. Or at least the trigger or something. It was just after Hurt shot her that the wave happened. I don't know, but her blood was on me when it hit. I did feel that woman I pulled out at the college and a lot of other people that were going through this hell. I don't think I really felt my own feelings then at all."

Toni picked up a file folder from the desk and said, "Follow me and keep quiet. Act like I'm still pissed at you."

"Are you?"

She didn't answer, she just walked out the door, leaving me to trail behind her looking at my feet. We wound around the back of the office and down the chain link to a cinder block wall with doors on either side. She unlocked and entered the fourth door on the right.

Kai still sat in the steel chair in the middle of the room. He wasn't taped or tied in any way, but there were no windows, and the vent was too small even for his scrawny ass. He saw me and immediately recoiled internally, but then put up a mask of bravado.

"Easy Kai," Toni said, "We're just here to talk."

"I'd ask for a lawyer, but I guess we're a little bit past the whole habeas corpus thing."

It might have been a good front, but I knew better. I felt his fear, his guilt. I could also feel his struggle. He was still going back and forth on whether he'd done the right thing. I remembered the feeling from my time in the corps. I squatted on my haunches a few paces away to reduce my threat level.

"I know where you're at, Kai," I told him, "Sometimes you get orders that didn't feel right. You follow them anyway. Then you have this struggle after deciding whether you'd done right. That's your struggle—but—I'm going to ask you to be honest with me now, and if you are, I will do what I can to see you don't get strung up for genocide and high treason."

"I will," Kai said after a moment, "But only to you. She has to go." We looked at Toni in unison, and she huffed, but conceded.

"Fine, but if you kill him and I get fired..." She pointed a finger first at me and then at Kai in warning, and then went out, shutting the door behind her. No doubt standing right there to listen as well as she could. I dragged a five-gallon bucket over to sit on, and waited for him to start. When he didn't, I offered a little prompt.

"You realize that whatever's left of the world will want someone's head for this. They'll probably mount it in the national museum."

"Yeah, I know. But what if they were right, Max?"

"How can you even ask that man? Look around you. Look at the bodies. Look at the children! Can you sit there and tell me that's right?"

"No, of course not."

"Then how can you still ask?"

"Because I saw all the bodies before. So did you. I also saw all the trees, fish, all the birds, and the elk dying. Max, I was a biologist before the war, man. I went to seven countries on three continents and both coasts of our own country. It was all dying. We were killing it. When Hurt came to me, I knew he was a lunatic, but he offered me a way to do something to stop it."

"You realize your part in this makes you a lunatic too, right?"

"Yeah. I do. I had no idea it would be like this. This bad. This big. Max, please believe I would never have done this if I knew. I felt like I was fighting again for something worthwhile. If society changed, if humanity changed, maybe we'd quit rushing everything to extinction."

"Well, now we're the ones going extinct. You've seen what's going on out there. There don't seem to be too many humans left, and those that are being hunted by—by what? Just what the hell did you guys do?"

"I don't exactly know. I never got too high in the ranks, but my basic understanding is that the spell creates a kind of genetic-level recombination. Not a splicing, but more a kind of chimerism. I don't know. It's magic, not science. Maybe that's the same on some level, but it's all so fucked up..." He was babbling, near hysterics. It seemed he'd come to a decision on whether they were right or wrong. "It was supposed to show us that we're all one."

"You know all that, but you don't know who was running the show?"

"Like I said, I only knew Hurt, but he indoctrinated people well. There were a shitload of us spies and cleaners. You might think this is over because you got Hurt and busted me, but he's just the little guy. A recruiter. These guys are so secretive, they don't even have a name."

"Sure they do."

"I never heard it."

"That's funny, because we've been calling them the Shadow Council."

"The guys from the letters? I guess I should have known. Too busy on the other stuff. Rumors among the spies said they were all corporate and government bigwigs, like that illuminati and Bilderberger crap the theorists were spouting a few years back. They say that these guys believe their own hype, though. That by culling the human herd and cultivating genetic diversity, they would promote global unity."

"Pretty good spiel, sounds like you bought it."

"I did. God forgive me, I did."

"How do we know you won't go off the res again if we let you go?"

"Because you have genocide and treason over my head, and I'll let you chip me. You'll know where I am all the time. I can attempt to re-infiltrate and you guys can check out all the places I go."

"You could still lead us on a snipe hunt," I said, but I could feel a real flutter of hope in him.

"My word. As a brother-in-arms."

"You betrayed the whole world."

"I know I'll never face a trial or a firing squad. Either you guys will kill me, or they will. Either way, I'd like to try to help stop them before I die."

"You screw me, and I'll squeeze the life out of you myself. And I'll enjoy it," I said, watching him slump further into the chair.

"Yeah. There's that."

I emerged from the room to find Toni leaning nonchalantly against the cinder block wall. I gave her a little grin and started walking back up the hall. This time it was her trailing behind, bewildered.

"So what do you think?" I stopped about halfway up and stepped aside to let her catch up with me.

"About what?"

"You know I know you were listening, right?"

"What— you can read minds too?"

"No, I can just tell by how you're feeling."

"You can get all that? Was he telling the truth?"

"From his point of view, yes. He will work for us if we let him, and he won't double-cross me." Toni stifled a laugh. I popped an eyebrow.

"You just used the term double-cross in a sentence. How very James Bond."

"Never. I drink my liquor straight."

"Okay, but that tequila crap is just nasty."

I was getting the idea that maybe, just maybe things could be alright again someday. That was when she tripped. Toni tripped over her own feet and had to scramble to catch the folder she'd been carrying before its contents went sprawling all over the floor.

A single piece of paper slipped out and floated in graceful arcs to the floor. I picked it up. We both looked at it. Then we looked at each other. Then we turned simultaneously and went back to the room. I swung the door open with Toni hot on my heels.

"Okay, Kai," I said, holding the slip of paper out to him. "You work for us starting now. What is this list?"

"It's a list of codes, I think. Hurt never really told me what it was." I didn't need empathy to see that Ben was having the same thought that had brought us back here. "Or code names," he said.

"Thank you!" I said, handing the list off to Toni and planting a Bugs Bunny kiss on the top of his head, "This might just save your ass, buddy."

"God, I hope it helps. I can never do enough." I noticed then that he'd been crying. I supposed the empathy only worked in close proximity. That thought helped immensely.

Dr. Pape was talking to someone on the radio when we got back to the office. I assumed at first it was the CB, but as she moved I could see that the CB was now sitting beside the newly-acquired HAM unit. She was smiling and saying how very pleased she was and that she would be anxiously awaiting their return.

"I am too," Arlan's voice responded, "I'll be bringing the helicopter back when I come, so we'll have a way to get above it all, so to speak."

"Wonderful Arlan," she said, "I'll talk to you when you get back." She turned around to address us next. "Well, I trust you have news?"

"Yeah," I said, "And you?"

"Yes." She said, sharing a sly look with us. "We have maintained continuity of government after a fashion. It is the former speaker of the house that is President now. In better news, Arlan has addressed the remaining members of Congress on our behalf, and in light of the current crisis, they have given The Office of Human Protection carte blanche.

We have access to whatever we need. Unlimited funding until the nation gets back on its feet. Our international allies are establishing offices as well. We are now a global entity. Roosevelt would be proud. Also we can start construction on the new facility as soon as we find a spot."

"I think I know just the spot," I said.

She beamed at me, and asked, "So what was your news?"

"This list of words," Toni said, handing her the slip, "We knew they weren't random. Now we're thinking they're code-names."

"Are we sure?"

"No, but Kai seems to think that might be what they are. Looking at them, it seems likely."

"The same Kai we just popped as a mole?" She looked at Toni now, severe in expression, "You let *him* in there with him?" Then she looked at me just as harshly, saying, "And do *you* still believe anything he says?"

"He's not lying. He knows he did wrong and wants to help. He didn't have any idea it was going to be like this."

"That doesn't matter! If you shoot someone, you don't get to say 'I didn't think they'd actually die' and make everything okay. What makes you so sure he's not lying now to save his own skin?"

"Apparently," I said looking at my shoes and trying not to feel her emotions, "I am an empath now."

"They're never going to gi..." She stopped. I looked up to see her blinking at me as if I'd just sprouted horns. She laid one hand on the desk and leaned into it a little. I wondered briefly if I had sprouted horns, then she redirected herself, saying, "You're an empath. That must be something."

"I can feel what people are feeling if I'm close to them, and it's getting stronger."

She found the desk chair and sat in it, saying, "I suppose this happened when everyone else started changing?"

"Yes ma'am."

"Who else knows about this?"

"Just her," I said twisting a thumb in Toni's direction, "and Daniel."

"That makes sense. And who all knows about this list?"

"Just Toni, Kai, me and you."

"Let's keep it just that way. Get Kai's allegiance in writing, and make him sign a full confession to his involvement. Let him know we can broadcast it to the public at any time and there will be nowhere to hide. I want him pinned down good."

"You're allowing this?"

"He hasn't been formally charged yet, and as long as this stays between the five of us, we should be able to control it."

"Seven," Toni said, "Donald and Arlan know we popped Kai, and what for. They don't have to know about Max though."

"No," I said. "Bring them in. Arlan seems to know his shit, and Daniel and Donald are going to be close. Let's not put that stress on them."

"If you say so," Pape said, "I think I'd like a word with our young man before I pardon him. And let's see if we can get a start on those code names, if that's what they are."

"If these are the names of the members of the Shadow Council, then we sh—" Toni started, but was interrupted by Dr. Pape.

"And let's find something else to call them, 'The Shadow Council' sounds like something out of a comic book, and it gives them too much credit."

Toni clammed up and we nodded. Pape motioned us to go and we left the office. The relief was immediate. I'd tried to block them but Dr. Pape had been giving off mixed emotions since we'd walked in on her conversation with Arlan. They'd swirled about her so fast I couldn't nail down anything specific. Maybe it was a woman thing.

"So now what?" Toni asked, looking out across the open front of the shop where new people were re-arranging the shelving and making places to put people and things.

"Well, we have a list of names and a place to be and food to eat. Lots of people don't have those things. Some of them aren't even human anymore, and some of them eat people. I guess we're pretty lucky."

"You know what we don't have?"

"What's that?"

"Any idea who the people are that belong to those names. We don't know who orchestrated this whole thing. We're not even one-hundred percent sure that this is a spell. That's just Arlan's hypothesis."

"Also Hurt's dead, but someone is still sending snipers. I don't think for a minute that was a random shooter on the bridge that shot Daniel. They know what we look like, and that we're still alive. Kai didn't feed them that info."

"Well, whether there's an actual spell or a science experiment, there is an organization. There are people who are responsible, and if they are still out there it is our responsibility to make sure they pay for it."

"If we're going to do that we have to find out where our other leak is."

"Other leak—" she said. "Oh."

"You know what else?" I could feel her anxiety mounting as we spoke. "How did Arlan get to DC so fast?"

She didn't reply. I glanced around to see if we were being noticed, but everybody was engrossed in what they were doing.

"Hey," I said, reaching out a hand to her, "I need to show you something."

TWENTY-SIX

I led Toni out the side of the parking lot and around the corner down 166. We went past the tree girl who smiled sleepily and crooned to a less-than-enchanted Toni, and then turned up the gravel drive to the barn. Keeping an eye out for centaurs and other stray creatures, I walked her right up to the doors.

"Well, what do you think?"

"It's gorgeous, but it's just an old barn. Why show me this?"

"Remember the barn in Maryland? This would be a pretty good entrance cover, wouldn't it?"

"You mean for The Office? Kind of exposed here isn't it?"

"Not really," I said, pushing open the big doors. "You put it underground like the one in Maryland, and leave the barn, maybe let the brush grow up around the entrance.

There's a great view down the hill from the loft, and there are already all kinds of antennas and stuff up here. It's just out of the way enough, and just industrial enough that the Steel plant and the barn make the perfect cover. Let's sink it right here. In the hill. Come on!"

I led her up the ladder and pushed open the big loft doors on either side. We looked out on one side over the railroad tracks and Frankhoma road. From here you could see almost all the way to 66. From the other side you could see the back of the steel shop and the series of repeaters and cell towers.

As she looked at it all, I could feel the ideas blossoming within her. That hope flutter was there, and that warmth I'd felt in her before. That desirous warmth I had a hard time ignoring.

"If we dig in sideways," I said, taking a step closer, "Tunnel over from the steel plant and reinforce..." I could smell her hair. I felt her respond to my closeness. It made breathing difficult and more important, as my head felt like it was trying to float off. My heart raced. I could hear her breath quicken as well.

She knew I could sense her, and now, she would know how I felt as well. I pulled her to me. Desire rolled off her in thick musky tendrils. I could feel them everywhere. Even as she tried to keep her hands in check, her need curled around me in the most intimate places. Places I hadn't thought of. As I felt her desire, it made me think of the same places on her body. What it would be to touch them, caress and kiss them.

I picked her up, holding her legs around my waist, feeling the heat of her against me, and carried her to the hay. When I touched her, I felt her pleasure, returned it, and felt it grow. Everything she gave me, I doubled and gave back. The sensations of lovemaking were enhanced a hundred-fold by the mingling of our emotions. The peaks were so high, I was lost, obliterated completely by her.

As I sat holding her afterward, looking out over the curve of the road at the foot of the hill below us and the rolling hills between here and Tulsa, something cold crept into the warmth between us. She was growing distant, pulling her emotions away from me. I was losing something precious and couldn't suss why.

"We can't do this," she said finally, stepping away.

"We already have."

"I mean this—relationship. We can't have a relationship."

"Who says? Aren't we a little beyond office politics?"

"Because," she said, a pang of guilt hitting her right at the solar plexus, "Because you have an unfair advantage and I can't let you use it against me."

"I wouldn't." The hurt was mine this time.

"You would. The first time you didn't get your way, or the first time I tried to keep a secret. The first time I had to reign you in, you would use my feelings for you to get your way."

"What makes you..."

"I've got to go," she said, standing to straighten her skirt, "And we probably shouldn't be alone together again. This was a mistake."

"No, it wasn't. Becoming this—feeling like this—it's changed me."

"We'll see." She disappeared down the ladder and left me there. I pulled on my pants and watched her disappear around the turn in the driveway.

It didn't make any sense. I'd have to figure it out later though, because the sun was going down, and people—or other things—would come looking sooner or later. It would be wise not to be out after dark. I gave her a few minutes to keep up appearances, and then I too climbed down the ladder and trudged up the hill. Suddenly the world was colder, darker. I looked up at the sky and realized it really had grown darker. The wind had picked up. I was so wrapped up in Toni, I hadn't noticed that a storm had been brewing. As I passed the tree girl, I noticed she was making a different sound. This was a sad singing or a soft keening. I'd gone a few steps past her, when I stopped in my tracks and backed up.

When the wind paused and no longer bent her to its will, she reached toward me. I wasn't feeling an emotion from her like before, but it seemed—she looked—like she felt sorry for me. I let her stroke my cheek with her thinning purple leaves, and then told her I had to go. *Have I worn it out? Can you use up empathy?* But another idea was trying to sneak in the back of my brain. What if I wasn't feeling her emotions because I was projecting my own and she was feeling them? What if I'd done the same thing to Toni? If I had, she'd be completely justified in what she'd said to me. I needed to talk to Daniel. Now.

By the time I made it back up the hill to the shop, the wind was howling and the temp must have been near freezing. Deep blue clouds hung low to the hill, reminding me of the ones from my vision. I ducked in the door just before the wind caught it and barely made it without getting slammed into. The lights were on. I hadn't heard a generator, but the noise may have been carried off by the wind.

I went to find Daniel. Daniel was over by the south wall, helping to offload a pallet of supplies they had just brought back. There were more people than ever, and the idea of being in close quarters with all of them was making me even more self-conscious than I already felt.

The smack of anger I caught from Daniel as he turned and saw me didn't help at all.

"What's wrong, Dan?"

"You know for an empath, you're kind of an asshole."

"Shh!" I chastised, "I don't want everyone to know. What the hell did I do now?"

"It's not what you've done, it's what you haven't."

"Get your hands dirty. Get to know people, help get this place in shape."

"Let me ask you something before I go do something about something," I said. Daniel looked both perplexed and agitated, and I felt those things just fine.

"Shoot," he said.

"Can empathy go both ways?"

"I don't really know. Telepathy does, so I guess it could. If it's basically the same."

"Therin could project some kind of energy into people she touched. Could this be like that?"

"I don't know," he said, "Let's find out." Before I realized what he was doing, he clapped a hand on my shoulder. Then his jaw dropped. "Oh my god, she dumped you." It wasn't a question.

"Shh. Again. Nobody's supposed to know."

"Sorry. That wasn't really a secret, though."

"Really?"

"Not even a little bit. And yes, your emotions are all out there. Overwhelming, in fact."

"Could it happen without a touch?"

"Maybe. If—man, I am so sorry, that really sucked. What happened?"

"I think I did something to her. I didn't mean to. When we—I mean... I think things got intense and I lost control of the shit. I felt what she was feeling and she felt what I was feeling—I think it scared her." Daniel's eyes seemed to glaze a bit. He was lost in thought for a moment.

"Contact-driven biofeedback loop," he said.

"Do huh?"

"Just like you were saying, your feelings intensified each others, it started a cycle between you that got more intense at every turn. It quit when you two..."

"Yeah."

"So there is a limit. At least in that scenario. You'll have to watch it, though. You could affect people left and right and not intend to. Especially if you can project without contact."

"So you're telling me I could hurt someone? I could be dangerous?"

"You have no idea."

I leaned in to whisper, "I can never have sex again?"

"Well," he said slyly, "Let's just say your relationships are going to have to be about more than just sex, and you're going to have to reign it in a bit. Or you'll have to be content with meaningless trysts."

"Complicated."

"Yeah, welcome to humanity—sort of. Are we done now? Some of us have actual work to do."

"Hey, somebody's got to be available for real agent stuff."

"Slacker."

"Wuss."

I walked to the back of the building and saw that Kai had been released. He was sitting on a rolling stepladder that resided along the wall. In front of him there was a group of people gathering around a TV they'd dug up somewhere and plugged in.

They gathered shoulder to shoulder, but I managed to squeeze in, trying not to let their emotions overwhelm me. Toni and Dr. Pape had noticed the gathering and come over to join. Toni stood a little apart, arms crossed.

There was a disheveled woman on the screen and she was reading off city and town names, each one followed by a number. Each number was in the tens of thousands. I was just getting the idea of what she was reading when she said it.

"Again, these are not the official death tolls. There are no official death tolls. They are just tallies from the remnants of local governments around the viewing area. The story is the same across the globe."

A ticker started running across the bottom of the screen, and a HAM frequency occupied the top right corner of the screen. "There will be no video, but we will continue to broadcast on this station as long as we can. We now return you to the available program." What replaced her after the screen went blank was a rerun of "The A Team." Not the movie, but the 80's TV show.

The ticker continued to scroll across the screen, and some were transfixed, but I couldn't stay there. Suddenly everything Daniel had said made sense. The only thing that we really needed to do right now was help others survive this and protect them. It was the job, now. Sure, there was a mole, and people were still out there bent on the destruction of the human race, but finding them was pointless if there was no one left to save. I strode out the door just in time to see Daniel backing up to head back into town.

"Still need extra hands?"

"Of course we do! Come on up!"

I jogged around to the passenger side and opened it. Donald scooted over to sit in the middle. *Oh, he's entirely too happy.* It was going to be an awkward ride.

By the time we made town, Donald had us both laughing so hard we were crying. There was no awkwardness. These guys were the shit. They were warm and fun. Nothing else mattered. It did occur to me that we could make more trips if we had more trucks, and it occurred to me that it was dark, freezing, and howling up a storm.

"You know, we could really use more trucks, don't you think?"

"It'd be nice, but *somebody'd* have to drive them," Daniel said, "And I'm not leaving this guy behind the wheel for a second."

"I'd drive one. You think you could drop me and one more at a yard or something?"

"Sure, There's the school lunch warehouse off 66 Westbound. That's our next stop. There should be trucks there. Plus there's a gas pump over by the city yard if we need to fill up."

"Sounds good." I didn't have the heart to ask him how he'd come to know all of this.

TWENTY-SEVEN

We made it to the school warehouse and retrieved not one, but two, which gave us three delivery trucks total. I would drive one, a man named Troy would drive another, and Donald would drive the third truck. We huddled around the map that Daniel produced, and decided to work the outskirts of town.

"We'll leave anything that looks inhabited alone," Daniel said, "And we'll work the institutions and businesses. Even if it's been looted, take a look. Stay sharp though, you never know what's going to come out of the woodwork, and the power's still down."

We separated, three people to a truck. One of the new recruits, a man named in his sixties or better named Ross and his wife, Cherie, were assigned to the truck I would drive.

Daniel grabbed the jack handle out of the truck and we went up to the warehouse doors. The big bay doors could probably be jimmied, but it might take both of us to do it. A big part of me felt like I was stealing, but I knew people needed to be fed, so I smacked the feeling down and went to help as he stuck the bar into the mechanism that held the door in its track.

We pulled together and metal squealed. We let up to give Daniel a chance to get a new bite on the door, and another sound, unmistakable, filled the night. It was the distinct clap-latch of a round being chambered in a pump action Mossberg, much like the one under the seat in Dan's truck. We all stopped and stood stock still.

Finally, I turned slowly. The walk-in door had opened while we were trying to open the big door. The Mossberg was levelled at me from the doorway. It was held there by a woman in a smart-looking suit and black, low-heel pumps. Her short dark hair, likely perfectly coiffed on a regular day, stuck out in clumps all over her head. Her eyes were wide, but the set of her jaw said she'd mow us down if we so much as twitched the wrong way. Fear hung thick around her—threatened to swallow her up—me too, if I let it.

"Oh," I said, trying to pretend I wasn't having bladder issues just then, "there *is* someone here. Sorry. We'll just leave you to it then." She didn't answer me directly. She looked past me to the people standing in the lot.

"You're all still human?"

"Last we checked."

"You're not one of those freak-things, are you?"

"No ma'am," I said, unsure if it was the truth in my case. "In fact, we're from The Office of Human Protection. Say, would you like to come with us? We're setting up a help center up on the hill."

"A help center? Are there more real people there?"

"Yes ma'am, that's what we're doing here. We were looking for food to feed the people."

"This food is for the school children."

"I understand," I told her, trying to match her slowing emotional spin. If I could project, maybe I could help keep us all from getting killed.

"We're just trying to get everything together, so folks don't have to wander around looking for things. It's kind of dangerous these days. Can I ask your name Ma'am?" I'd matched her vibe and was slowing mine little by little. Hers seemed to come down with me.

"If it means you'll quit calling me 'ma'am,' it's Janene. Janene Somers."

"Well we can leave it, but it sure would help a lot of people, and the power isn't coming back soon, so all that stuff in the freezer would go south. We could sure use the help..."

She didn't move for a moment, but she was still coming down with me, and seemed to be thinking it over. She also seemed to be feeling better.

"Well, you might as well back those trucks up to the ramps," she said, lowering the shotgun and holding up the keys to the building, "It'll take a lot less time. I can't come with you, I have to see if I can find my sister if she's still alive. If you guys have got this. I can go. There's a map of all the drop sites on the office wall. Take care of my kiddos."

"Will do. Are you sure?"

"She's the only family I have." She patted me on the shoulder and said as she went past me, "You know, I'm really surprised nobody else has showed up."

She made her way down the deep stone steps and got into her Toyota and drove into the night with her shotgun in her lap. I shook my head, and then started unlocking doors. We got the trucks backed in and loaded, and Daniel had the map from the office rolled up beside him.

Our standoff with Janene had taken some time, so we decided to head back up the hill and set out again at first light.

My truck was in the lead, Donald was behind me, and Daniel was bringing up the rear when we pulled out of the parking lot. We'd gone up 66 (now Dewey Street) to Main and were just in the process of turning the corner when three people ran across the road right in front of me.

I hit the brakes, but still almost didn't stop in time. I heard the brakes of the truck behind me lock up, and hoped they could stop in time to keep from knocking me into them.

The people kept running. They hardly even seemed to notice they'd almost been run over. When they got to the other curb, the last two of them fell, one tumbling over another, and I could see that it was a girl and a boy.

They weren't looking at me though, they were watching the pack of werewolf looking creatures closing in for the kill.

I flung the shifter into park and my door open. There were protests from inside the cab, but I paid them no heed as I hoofed it over to the pair and scooped up the boy. I grabbed the girl's hand and tugged her along as I ran back to the truck. I stuffed the boy up into the cab and then the girl, and they slid over to sit by Ross and Cherie.

I got in and slammed the door behind me, hoping that I hadn't just doomed us all. The creatures didn't exactly get out of the way as I put the truck into gear and began trundling through the intersection, uphill. They snapped and swiped. They snarled and drooled, but seemed unsure whether they wanted to take on the trucks.

The creature that had been in the lead when they arrived lunged at the truck just as I got it into second. I could hear the other trucks going through their own shift patterns. Something smashed into the side of the truck. One of the creatures presumably, and then the leader jumped again, this time catching the passenger side mirror and hanging on. There were more thumps as the others joined in. There was a thud in the back and then a moment later something was scrabbling across the top of the truck. The leader was snarling and snapping at the passenger window where the others had been huddled moments before. Now they leaned over, almost in my lap as I struggled beneath bodies to shift into third.

The thing from the top jumped down onto the hood. The face might once have been human, but no longer held any trace of feeling. There was only hunger. It was blocking most of my view of the road.

I had to get it off the hood. The leader proceeded to hit the glass on his window. I swerved. The thing on the hood slid, but grabbed the wiper housing at the last minute. It snapped its jaws full of jagged, not quite human teeth, and its wild eyes darted back and forth across the cab from person to person, deciding perhaps, who he wanted to eat first.

Then, as we topped the hill, I worked the wheel back and forth swerving to try and shake one of them. They hung on with grim determination. There was no way to get them off before we got to the shop. I prayed no one would come out to meet us. We pulled in and spread out as much as we could.

The door opened. Light flashed across the parking lot and Toni stepped out of the shop. I was helpless. If I opened the door, they would be on me.

If I rolled down the window, they would have all of us. I laid on the horn. Soon the other trucks followed suit. Her face registered confusion, and then her eyes widened in surprise as the leader peeled off of the mirror and leapt at her. He covered the space before she could do much, and was on her, knocking her to the ground. Two pops. Two twitches and it was over. Dr. Pape raised one elegant eyebrow as she peered over the pistol sights. Others came out shooting and in a moment the beast on the hood exploded into a spray of blood and gore that covered the windshield.

Soon, everything stopped. Before we were sure enough to open them, the doors opened and people were helping Ross, Cherie and the kids out of the truck. Dr. Pape opened my door and stood there with a look, saying simply, "Why am I not surprised?"

I got out and around the door just in time to see Toni emerging from beneath the creature that had led the pack. She'd shot it and it landed on her. I went over and helped her up, looking her all over all at once.

"Gods, let me look at you, are you alright?"

She brushed herself off and picked a bit of monster out of her hair that was falling charmingly around her shoulders. She gave me a shove on the shoulder.

"Of course I'm alright. Arlan saved my life."

"Arlan?" I followed her gaze and saw the old guy standing in front of the helicopter on the roof in his tacky Hawaiian shirt and flip flops. In October. I gave him a smile and a wave.

Arlan shouldered his rifle and waved back and called down, "I'm glad to see you found some more trucks, we're going to need them! I have wonderful news, meet me inside!"

Toni huffed and strode away, giving off nothing more than annoyance at my continued presence in her world. I wished I hadn't, but I'd felt other things when I helped her up. I'd felt her shame, and worse—her fear of me. This damage I'd never be able to undo. By acting without knowing the limits of my abilities, I had hurt someone I cared about. Again.

I put my head down and followed her, feeling a lot like a dirty spy. When we got inside, Arlan was just coming in the back way. He was grinning from ear to ear, but waited for Dr. Pape and the others to join us.

"There is great and terrible news," he began, "You all probably know the terrible news, our world has been forever changed. Most of humanity is in ruins. What remains may or may not be human, and those that are may not stay that way. Small pockets of survivors are scattered around everywhere, but are only just surviving at the moment. The good news is that the combined resources of the United States government are at our disposal as we build the new facility for The Office of Human Protection. Those of you who wish to stay as employees can begin signing up tomorrow. The rest of you will be our guests here until we get shelters set up in town. We have a blank check, so-to-speak. We begin as soon as a location is found."

A twitter of excitement went around the room and I raised my hand.

"I think I have a place."

"Well done, my boy. You can tell us all about it in the office," Arlan said, "The rest of you can decide what you desire and let us know in the morning."

As people dispersed, I followed Dr. Pape and her entourage back to the little office. Though we all spread out to face the center of the room, I felt all eyes on me.

"Well," Arlan said, "Let's have it, my boy, where is it?"

"It's right behind you." I felt Toni bristle, but continued. "We can dig under the barn at the top if the hill behind us. Dig across and then straight down. The entire operation would be underground and out of sight. The only people that know where it is being built will be us and the people working on it. If we have a mole, it's one of us. The list will be short and easy to sort out."

"That's great, Max," Dr. Pape said. I wasn't sure if she was being sarcastic, if she was still annoyed with me, or both, but things were still pretty hostile. I wondered if the ladies had discussed what happened between Toni and I. Suddenly I felt very exposed. Then she said, "Where did you come up with that?"

I felt the lurch of guilt and shame in Toni and wanted to cry. "When I took off and raided the bar, I had to hide in the loft from the centaurs. I saw the antennas and stuff sticking up and thought we could use this place without anyone in town being the wiser. We could hide in plain sight."

"We'll certainly give it some thought," Dr. Pape returned, and Arlan nodded enthusiastically, "Keeping things close seems to be prudent just now."

"Thanks," I said simply, and then nodded to them and walked out.

Toni followed me out to the common area that was taking shape where all the shelves had been. When I sat at one of the little folding tables, she sat across from me.

"Thank you for not ratting me out back there," she said. Straightforward and no sugar. That was Toni.

"What was I going to say? You were pretty clear about how you felt. I'm not that vengeful."

"I know. I just wanted to say thanks. And I'm sorry."

"You don't have anything to be sorry about, I do."

"I'm still sorry, and I still feel the same. We can't happen."

"I know. It's all right," I said. "I'm going to take the motorcycle and drive into Tulsa and check on the woman from the college. You want to come?"

"At night? No. And alone with you, no. You go if you feel like you have to, but be careful. She needs someone to look after her."

Her unspoken message was clear. She didn't need me.

"You know," I said, "She would have kicked that werewolf-thing's ass if she had some training. She fought like a wild thing. And there was something about her. That vision..."

"What vision, Max?"

"Nothing," I said, "Nevermind. You have a good night. Really. We're fine. I may crash at the Hospital for the night, see if they need help."

"Be careful Max," she said.

I grunted a response as she walked away. There was nothing I could do. Nothing except go and be there for someone who did need someone. I got onto the bike and turned the handlebars toward Tulsa. Maybe those cases were still in the back of that bar. That would make for handsome accompaniment at the hospital. Maybe I'd just stay there until the woman from the college woke up. I never even looked in her purse to find her name. I twisted the throttle and eased her out of the parking lot. It was time to go find out her name. Then it was going to be time to get to the bottom of this shit for once and for all.

Fin.

(The Nova Chronicles Continue in Book 2: Nova Wave)

Excerpt from *Nova Wave*, Chapter 1

It was almost exactly like you'd expect, except I didn't die. It was a close thing, and maybe looking back I wish I had, but for now, just know that it was too good to be true. The beautiful starlit night, a nip in the October air, and a gorgeous full moon...this was a night college girls dreamt of. It's also the last night I remember of 2017.

About the Author

D.E. Chandler lives in Sapulpa, Oklahoma with her husband, Tom. When she's not writing, she enjoys reading, learning, and being in Nature. She maintains a website, dechandlerwrites.com where you can view some of her other works and keep up with news about the writing. She is also available on Facebook, Twitter, Instagram and Pinterest.

Look for the new short story, "Her Last Question" in the upcoming anthology, *Blackbird's Third Flight*!

Made in the USA
San Bernardino, CA
16 January 2017